OCEAN OF FEAR

BOOK SIX OF THE KORMAK SAGA

WILLIAM KING

Typhon Press Limited
GLASGOW, SCOTLAND

* * *

MORE BOOKS BY WILLIAM KING

Stealer of Flesh

Defiler of Tombs

Weaver of Shadow

City of Strife

Taker of Skulls

Born of Darkness

Sword of Wrath

Masque of Death

CHAPTER ONE

FEET THUNDERED ACROSS the trireme's deck as the crew raced to their battle stations. Drums sounded the beat for the straining oarsmen. Marines strapped on shields and drew shortswords. Crossbowmen wound their arbalests and fitted bolts into place. Sweating and puffing, the engine crew on the sterncastle manoeuvred the ballista to cover the shoreline.

Standing at the prow of the warship above the great beak of the ram, the tall greying man watched the distant village burn. A frown made his scarred face even more sinister. He shaded his cold grey eyes against the sea glare and studied the devastated little township on the forest's edge.

Smoke rose above the huts and fires crackled along the wooden palisade. Dead bodies, some pierced with arrows, sprawled on the sand of the beach. He could make out no sign of life.

He walked back towards the stern. Superstitious sailors avoided his glance and made the Sign of the Sun when they thought he would not notice. They knew what sort of man carried a sword on his back. They knew why he was aboard and they did not like it. Since he had joined the ship three days ago in the northern Siderean port of Grahal, he had done nothing but make them uneasy.

As the man approached the sterncastle the ship's captain broke off his discussion with the chaplain and nodded permission to join him on the command deck. "You may come up, Sir Kormak," he said.

Kormak stalked up the stairs and studied the captain. Elias Zamara, by Grace of King-Emperor Aemon of Siderea, Captain of the Ocean's Blade and admiral of this small pirate-hunting fleet, was almost as tall as Kormak, with the copper-blond hair and hawk-like features of a Siderean nobleman. He wore the elaborate ruffled collar and purple cloak of the royal court. A gold Elder Sign with three interlocked five-pointed stars hung on his chest like a badge of office. His manner was supercilious; the easy way he strode the command deck said that he was not a man to be taken lightly.

"Have we found what we are looking for?" Zamara asked. His haughty tone could not hide his nervousness. Distant cousin to the king or not, Elias Zamara was still a young man with no great experience in dealing with sorcery, no matter how many sea battles he had fought in.

"Too early to say," said Kormak. "All I can see is a burned out village. Could be anything from Thurian raiders to an attack by elves who resent their lands being colonised."

"They were most likely only heretics anyway," said Frater Jonas. He gestured at the village as if condemning every soul in it to eternal damnation under the Shadow. The fleet's chaplain was a short bird-like man with very black hair, very dark eyes and a neatly clipped spade beard. His olive skin, darker than the captain's, made it clear that he belonged not to his country's Sunlander nobility but to its peasantry.

Jonas wore the yellow robes of the Order of the Eternal Sun, an organisation said to wield power second only to the King-Emperor in

Siderea. His hand stroked the solar emblem of his Order the way a man might a favourite cat. "They come here with their foul ways to escape the Holy Sun's sight."

The young nobleman looked at him with distaste, nor perhaps so much for the sentiments expressed but for the peasant accent they were expressed in.

"Someone certainly wanted them dead," Kormak said. "The question is why."

"There's only one way we're going to find out," said the captain. "We're going to have to send in a landing party."

"Very well," Kormak said. "Let's go take a look."

***

Scores of armed warriors from each of the fleet's three ships filled the rowboats. Some of the marines rowed the small craft towards the strand. Others pointed their cocked crossbows in the direction of the beach.

Elias Zamara sat with his hand on his sword's hilt. Frater Jonas clutched his Elder Sign as if it too was a weapon. He clearly expected some emissary of the Shadow to be waiting within the village to challenge his faith.

The marines kept their eyes fixed on the shore. They had the look of the typical Siderean professional soldier—stocky, dark-haired, medium height, olive-skinned. They were the same hardy breed that freed their country from the Seleneans and who were now spreading Siderean power across the Dragon Sea and the archipelagos of the World Ocean. Some said they were the best infantrymen the world had seen since the days of the Solari Legions and so far Kormak had found no reason to doubt that assessment.

The wind carried the smell of burned flesh, mingling it with the salt tang of the sea. The waves turned to white foam as they hit the sand and withdrew.

Kormak was the first to vault into the surf. Salt water wet him up to his thighs. Sand crunched beneath his boots. He made his way ashore as quickly as he could, uncomfortable with the way the water slowed his movements even for those few moments.

Silence brooded over the village. Gulls pecked at the corpses on the beach. Larger carrion birds fluttered skywards as they noticed the soldiers.

Kormak walked over to the nearest body. The dead woman's skirt had been raised above her waist. Blood pooled between her legs. Someone had raped her then stabbed her through the heart.

A man lay nearby, his throat cut. Maybe he had been forced to watch the woman die before they killed him. Kormak fought to keep his mind from constructing narratives. It was all too easy to picture what had happened here. He had seen the like many times, the first when he had been eight years old and it had been his own people dying.

Two children lay nearby. They stared up at the sky with blank empty eyes. Their throats had been cut too. They bore a family resemblance to the man and the woman.

"It was a mercy," said one of the soldiers. "The tykes would have starved to death without their folks to feed them." He did not sound as if he believed it. He sounded like he was trying to comfort himself.

The state of the corpses and the fact that the fires still burned made it obvious the attack was recent, most likely last night, possibly even some time before the dawn.

The slow burn of an anger that he knew, given time, would become incandescent fury started in Kormak's gut. He felt, as he always did, the need to make someone pay for this.

He unclenched his fists, took a deep breath and forced the rage down into the place where he had buried it long ago. A man in his line of work could not afford to give in to every spark of righteous anger. It was not his job to avenge these people. His duty was to find the sorcerer men called the Kraken and end his unrighteous career. Anything else was just a distraction.

"Silence," said Zamara with the chill authority of the Siderean nobleman. "No talking. There may be enemies watching us even now."

Frater Jonas bent over the children, made the Sign of the Sun, and then closed their eyes with surprising gentleness. He noticed Kormak looking at him.

"What?" he said.

Kormak responded to the harshness in his voice. "I thought they were only heretics."

Zeal and humanity warred on the priest's face. Humanity gained the upper hand, and Kormak found he liked the little man more for it. "Maybe so, but they were men and women, aye, and children..."

"Look at their faces," someone said, despite Zamara's order. Kormak understood what he meant. Terror twisted many of the dead's features. It was hardly surprising under the circumstances but clearly the men found it uncanny. They were ready to be spooked at the slightest thing. The soldiers knew they hunted a mage.

The gates of the village had been torn off their hinges. More bodies sprawled in the earthen streets. The small huts had been burned. The large central communal hall, possibly a temple of some kind, was now only smouldering wreckage. Vultures rose from their feasts and flapped slowly away, as if too gorged to fly any faster.

"The attack came from the beach," said Zamara. "No sign of

assault from the forest. I think it's safe to say this was the work of pirates."

"But was it the pirates we're looking for?" said Kormak.

"Split up! Search this place! Don't wander out of earshot," said Zamara. "See what you can find, though I doubt there will be anything. This place never had much to start with and it's been picked clean. But look anyway!"

"I'll need a party of men to gather up the bodies and prepare them for burning," said Frater Jonas. "I'll speak the rites myself."

"Of course, Frater," said Zamara. In the face of the death surrounding them, the mask of contempt had dropped from his face. He pointed to half a dozen men and said, "Gather the corpses."

He selected half a dozen more. "Gather wood and prepare a pyre. We can spare some oil from the ship to send these people into the Light."

Kormak was surprised. It was not the sort of wasteful gesture he would have expected from the young and ambitious Siderean nobleman.

"Sir," said one of the soldiers who had fanned out through the village, a grizzled veteran named Terves. "You had better see this."

His words were addressed to the captain but his eyes were on Kormak.

"Lead on, Terves," said the captain.

The soldier brought them to the corpse. It lay near the wall, in the shadow of the forest's edge.

"I've never seen anything like it," he said and then clamped his lips shut, as if sorry he had spoken.

"I have," said Kormak. The body looked desiccated. The skin had an ashen quality to it. The eyes were like shrivelled black olives. The flesh was flaking away. His mind drifted back to a dead child in the cold northlands of Taurea. Someone else he had been too late to save. Once more he found himself pushing his anger down.

"It looks like a mummy," said Zamara. "I saw things like this south of the Dragon Sea, in the Necropolis in Umbrea."

Terves nodded agreement. Kormak guessed both the captain and the old soldier had served time as part of the Siderean army holding the forces of Shadow at bay in that distant land.

"It's no mummy," said Kormak. "It's dressed like a villager."

"Look at it. It's been dead for centuries," said Zamara. He clearly wanted to believe that.

"It's certainly dead," said Kormak. "Most likely since last night."

"Then we've found what we're looking for," the captain said.

"I think so, yes," said Kormak. He bent down to inspect the corpse.

"When did you see the like?" Terves was white-faced but needed to ask. Zamara clearly wanted to know the answer as well for he said nothing to shut the man up.

"A few years ago along the edge of the Barrow Hills in Taurea, a wight had taken a child..."

"You think this was a wight?" Zamara asked, torn between disbelief and dread. Kormak shook his head.

"Wights rarely move from the places their bodies were interred, and there is no history of Kharonian barrow builders along the Blood Coast."

"Who knows what lies back there in the forest," said the soldier. "Those are elfwoods. The Old Ones dwelled there once. And some of them dwell there still."

"I suspect it was something that feeds in the same manner as a wight," Kormak said. He looked up. Zamara's hand clutched the triple Elder Sign at his throat. Terves made the Sign of the Sun over his heart.

"Feeds?" The captain's voice was flat. He was holding his fear under a tight rein.

"They devour the souls of their victims, consume their life force. Something has done the same thing here."

"I heard the Kraken was a sorcerer but this is like something you expect from the worst sort of Shadow worshipper."

"It may not have been him," Kormak said. "Perhaps he has bound a soul-eater to his service. Some sorcerers do."

Terves let out a small scared groan. His face was stony. If Kormak had not heard the sound he would not have known the man was afraid.

"In the name of the Light what manner of man are we hunting for?" Zamara asked.

"A very bad one," Kormak said. "One who deserves to die."

"If man he is, sir," said Terves.

"Man or demon, this will kill him," Kormak said, touching the hilt of the dwarf-forged blade that protruded over his left shoulder.

A noise from the far side of the village drew their attention. Frater Jonas came striding up. "It appears we have some survivors," he said.

"Let's see what they can tell us," Captain Zamara said.

CHAPTER TWO

A WOMAN, A teenage boy and a couple of children stood there, garbed in clothes made from a mix of buckskin and old sailcloth. Their faces were soot smudged. Their eyes were wide and fearful. They looked at the armed men surrounding them in abject terror, all except the boy. He looked angry.

"What happened here?" Zamara demanded. "Tell us!"

"There's nothing to be afraid of," said Frater Jonas. "The King of Siderea has sent us. We are here to protect you."

They looked from the tall nobleman to the small priest and they seemed more afraid of Jonas than Zamara. It was his robes, Kormak realised. They were heretics of some sort.

"The writ of the King-Emperor don't run here," said the boy. His fists clenched. "The Blood Coast is not part of Siderea."

"King-Emperor Aemon's word is law wherever his soldiers are," said Zamara. His manner was lordly but not unkind. "You'd do well to remember that, boy, before you speak."

The boy glared at him. Kormak recognised the belligerence in him. The youth had looked on horrors. He no longer cared what he said or what might be done to him.

"What is your name, lad?" Kormak asked before matters could spiral out of hand.

"You're no Siderean," the boy said. "You don't look like one. You don't sound like one."

"He asked you a question," Zamara said.

"I'm an Aquilean," Kormak said. He kept his voice gentle and moved between the soldiers and the survivors. "It's far north east of here."

"You don't sound like a barbarian." The boy seemed determined to give offence. "You sound like a priest."

"I was educated by the Order of the Dawn," Kormak said. The woman perked up.

"You're a Guardian then, a monster hunter," she said. "I thought as much from the way you carry that blade."

Her voice was not what Kormak had expected. It was aristocratic in its way. Perhaps she was one of those who sought sanctity in a simple way of life.

The boy seemed to have found something to hold on to now. "A monster hunter, eh? Well, there's work for you here!" His voice rose as he spoke till he was almost shouting.

"I thought there might be," said Kormak. "Why don't you tell me what happened?"

***

The boy's name was Lorenzo. The woman's name was Mora. The children were Edwin and Kaili. Their village had been known as Wood's Edge. It was a peaceful place, founded by Preacher Thomas to enable its folk to explore the simple glories of the Holy Sun away from the corruption and hypocrisy of the big cities and the Universal Church.

Last night a ship had been sighted out at sea, a long sleek vessel, a warship of sorts, flying the flag of Siderea, but not looking much like any royal ship the former sailors among the congregation could recognise. It was too stripped down, too long, too lean. Brother Herman who had a questionable past before he found the Light claimed it was a pirate vessel out of Port Blood. Its sails bore the mark of a Black Kraken, an ominous sign indeed.

The men who had put ashore bore no resemblance to royal sailors. They wore a motley assembly of tunics, head-bands and lace finery that might have come from some wealthy nobleman's chest. They carried well-oiled weapons. Their leader was a tall, regal looking man with a hatchet-face like that on Siderean coinage.

In the king's name he demanded to be let in and given food and water. The Preacher refused and that's when the Black Priest stepped forward at a command from the pirate leader.

Perhaps stepped was the wrong word. He glided, as if his feet did not quite touch the ground. His robes were black. The folds of his sleeves hid his hands. A cowl obscured his face. He spread his arms, emitted eerie sounds in a language that did not sound human. Demons came, like mist taking solid form out of the cold night air. They passed over the walls in a mass of swirling tentacles and terrifying features that the survivors could not quite recall.

The gate buckled at the Black Priest's touch. The pirates entered Wood's Edge and worked their will on villagers too terrified to resist. Lorenzo and his mother had somehow found themselves at the edge of the wood, leading the children under the shadow of the trees. They had cowered there, listening to the screams and howls of terror until they stopped and the pirates departed. They emerged to see if they could find any survivors and hid again when the three Siderean ships showed up this morning.

"When did the pirates go?" Kormak asked.

"They camped in the village overnight and they left with the dawn," said the boy. "I crept along to Headland Point and watched them set out from the woods there. They took the prisoners with them."

"Prisoners?" Kormak asked.

"Some of the older people. The Preacher."

"That makes no sense," said Zamara. "Slavers take men in their prime and young women. That's not what happened here."

"I know who they took," the boy said. "I saw them go."

"Which way?" Zamara asked. "Out to sea—towards the Sunset Islands?" It was a way of asking whether they had sailed west.

The boy shook his head. "They went upriver."

The captain looked at him open-mouthed. "Upriver. Are you sure?"

"Yes—they had oars out and they went up against the current. It was not what I would have expected either."

The captain shook his head. "That can't be right."

The woman said, "It is right. We watched them carefully. You would too, if your life depended on it."

"Why would they do that?" Frater Jonas asked.

"You would need to ask them," Lorenzo said. "I just know that's the way they went."

"What's up river?" Kormak asked.

"Elves," said the boy. "And a lot of them. We used to see them watching us from the edge of the forest."

"They ever attack you?"

"Why should they? We never attacked them and we always

respected the woods. The Preacher made us."

"Then we've caught him," said Jonas. "All we need to do is wait here and we'll catch him when he comes back downriver."

"If he comes back downriver," Kormak said.

"He has to," said Zamara.

"We can't be certain of that. There are two more estuaries within a score of leagues from here. Your own charts show that. How do we know that those rivers are not connected? They might be able to take another route back."

"We could split the fleet and cover the river mouths," said Frater Jonas.

The captain shook his head. "It would surrender our main advantage. We have three ships to his one."

"We could follow him upriver," said Kormak. He watched the captain make some calculations in his head.

"The Marlin and the Sea Dragon are ocean-going cogs converted for war. They draw too deep to go far upriver. Only the Ocean's Blade could follow under oar."

"And we would surrender our advantage," said Frater Jonas.

"Not necessarily," said Zamara. "We could pack the ship with marines. We'd have a numerical advantage in fighting men."

"You'd need to carry supplies as well."

"We have the supplies, Frater, and we could put the men on half-rations."

"Are you seriously considering following this pirate upriver?"

The captain nodded. "There's a chance we may overhaul him and take him by surprise. And it certainly beats waiting here for an indefinite period of time for a foe that might never come back this way. Who might even get lost in the jungle."

Zamara was convincing himself. He was one of those officers who preferred glory to waiting. And the Kraken had a large bounty on his head. This expedition might make Zamara's fortune if he was successful.

"We can leave the other two ships here to blockade the river mouth in case, he somehow slips past us."

He began to shout orders. Within ten minutes the village was clear and men and provisions were being transhipped to the Ocean's Blade. The survivors refused to leave their village. Kormak wondered what would become of them.

**

Kormak stood on the prow of the ship once more, studying the forest as it glided by. At this point the nameless river was wide and slow. A sailor with a plumb-line stood nearby measuring the depth and counting it off.

The Guardian wondered what would happen if the river became too shallow to navigate or was blocked by some obstacle. He consoled himself with the thought that anything that could impede the progress of the Ocean's Blade would also stop the pirate as well.

Or would it? The Kraken was a sorcerer and now there was this Black Priest to consider as well. He had asked the survivors about his magic but he had not got any more out of them than from his initial questioning.

Sandaled footsteps from behind him told him that Frater Jonas was approaching. The sailors all went barefoot, the marines wore boots and the captain had a heavier stride.

"Are you sure this is a good idea?" the priest asked in a confidential tone. He studied the undergrowth by the riverbank with nervous eyes. He ducked his head as the ship swept through a curtain of vines.

"No," Kormak said. "But what else could we do? Wait for the Kraken to come back? He might never do that."

"You really think there's an alternative route."

"He might be wiped out. The elfwoods can be a hostile place for mortal men."

"You sound as if you have had experience of that."

"I have."

A movement among the trees got his attention. Something was there, among the shadows. A deer emerged.

"I doubt we are going to be so lucky as to find the forest has swallowed our prey."

"I fear you are correct."

"It seems strange that a salt water pirate like the Kraken should suddenly decide on a river voyage."

"It seems strange to me that a sorcerer should turn pirate and start raiding the coasts of Siderea," Kormak said. "But it has happened. It's why I am here. The Trefal Merchant's Guild made a sizeable donation to my Order to ensure it."

"You think there is a connection between the Kraken being a sorcerer and this little excursion through elf country?"

"Terves was right—we have no idea what is really up here. There could be anything within these woods. They stretch hundreds of miles east of here, all the way to Taurea, and no man has ever crossed them."

"Or has at least recorded the tale, you are right about that. I've heard stories of everything being up here from giant walking trees to a lost city of the Old Ones."

The water swirled by the prow of the ship. The sweeps moved in time to the drumbeat. Frater Jonas stood by his side in companionable silence till eventually the Guardian spoke, "He's here for a reason. He has to be. Why come all this way otherwise."

"This Black Priest—what do you think he is?" There was a curious edge to Jonas's voice.

"I don't know. It may be an Old One bound to service by soul pact or it may be an apprentice."

"A strange apprentice who seems more powerful than most masters."

Kormak tilted his head and stared at Jonas. The little priest smiled. "Magic is studied openly in Siderea, Sir Kormak, and I have found it necessary to learn about it. Sorcery is no easy thing to work. To so swiftly summon the sort of creatures this one did beggars belief. An archmage would struggle to do such a thing and, thank the Light, there are few of those in this world. If this being is as powerful as those poor people implied I fear even you, with your formidable blade and your formidable talents, might struggle to overcome it. And it is the servant..."

"Is it?" Kormak said.

"Ah, now that is an interesting question," said Frater Jonas. "Perhaps the man we are pursuing is not the one we want at all. Perhaps it is this Black Priest, although I suspect priest is very much the wrong word to describe him."

Kormak studied the priest. He was taking all of this rather too well. Most priests would have been filled with righteous fury or simple terror at the thought of what the Kraken and his companion had done. "You may be right," Kormak said.

Frater Jonas made a small grimace that might have been a smile.

"Blessings of the Light upon you, brother," he said then he bowed and made the Sign of the Sun before he walked away.

CHAPTER THREE

"I NOTICE YOU were chatting with our ship's chaplain earlier," said Captain Zamara. He used his handkerchief to wave away the cloud of midges that floated above the river in the early evening light. Kormak wondered if he should be flattered at the captain descending from the command deck to speak with him.

"I suspect he is more than the ship's chaplain." Kormak said.

"You are a perceptive man." There was just the faintest hint of irony in the captain's voice. Zamara walked over to the man checking the plumb-line. He counted to himself, making sure the sailor was doing his job correctly. He walked back over to Kormak, leaned against the deck rail and said, "Frater Jonas is a spy and something more, I think. He has a reputation at court for being an expert on occult matters."

"You think he is a sorcerer?"

"The good Frater was an inquisitor before he took up his position as spiritual advisor at the Imperial Palace. He hunted witches and burned malefactors."

Kormak nodded. Perhaps it was not just Jonas's accent that made Zamara dislike him. Inquisitors were feared. In Siderea, even the mightiest might be brought down by an accusation of witchcraft.

Zamara said, "He was assigned to me as fleet-chaplain just before we departed on this mission. He had been with us only a few days longer than you have."

"As chaplain? Not as an inquisitor?"

"Exactly so."

"From the Palace Imperial to the under-decks of a warship in a few days. That is a big change."

Zamara's lips quirked into a humourless smile. "Perhaps he has displeased his superiors. Or the King-Emperor."

"Or perhaps there is another reason," said Kormak.

"Perhaps. Rumour has it that our Frater Jonas reports only to the head of his Order and the King-Emperor himself. His Order has tentacles everywhere. The tip concerning the Kraken's course and heading came from their agents."

Kormak considered this but said nothing.

Zamara remained quiet for a few heartbeats then said, "I disliked having him aboard as much as I disliked having you foisted on me. I confess that since hearing that boy's tale of demons I am rather glad you are both here. Cold steel, wild seas and decks awash with gore I do not mind. Sorcery sets my blood to freezing and this Black Priest... I like not the sound of him at all."

Zamara fell silent and stared out into the gathering gloom. He seemed to making some form of judgement as he watched the waters of the river flow sluggishly by. He nodded to himself, said something to the man with the plumb-line and said, "Good evening, Sir Kormak."

The captain withdrew to the sterncastle, wrapped himself in his cloak and took a seat in the great wooden chair beside the steersman's wheel. As Kormak watched, Terves brought him a cup of hot wine.

Kormak put his back against the guard-rail and closed his eyes. The day had given him much to think about and it was time to take his rest.

***

A scream rang out through the night. Kormak woke to the sound of thrashing on the deck and a horrible crunching noise. He rose to his feet. A massive form moved nearby, scales catching the lantern light. A screaming man's head protruded from a mound of what looked like cables. A cracking sound told of the man's ribs being broken.

A ghost snake, Kormak thought, one of the great forest constrictors. It must have dropped from the trees above and enveloped the struggling marine. Other soldiers dithered around the enwrapped man. They ran to and fro, panicked, not realising what was happening, fearing that a demon had emerged from the forest to claim their souls.

Kormak sprang to his feet. His blade slid from the scabbard. He aimed just below the reflected glitter of the lantern light in the creature's eyes, hoping to sever its head. At the last moment, as if sensing its danger, the snake unwound from around its prey. The dwarf-forged blade slid through the great coils of muscle in its lower body.

The creature hissed and thrashed in agony. Its muscular length hit one of the hanging lanterns, knocking it from its post. The lantern crashed to the deck, spilling oil and then igniting it. A stream of flame flowed across the deck, giving sudden flickering illumination to the scene.

Men shrieked when they saw the gigantic serpent and the flopping corpse of its victim revealed in the firelight. They threw themselves away from the monster. Some dived into the water.

Sailors bellowed with fear of another sort, the age-old terror of unleashed fire that every nautical man dreaded. The ship's decks and ropes were caulked with tar. Sailors kept their pigtails in place with it. The pitchy stuff burned all too easily.

The monster twisted to face Kormak, long neck rising out of a mound of coils. Its head swayed from side to side. Its forked tongue flickered as if tasting the air. The snake's upper body reached to almost twice Kormak's height. Stretched out, the thing might be half as long as the ship.

Zamara yelled from the command deck and the sailors responded to the authority of his voice. A man picked up a bucket of water and rushed towards the flames, tossing the contents into their midst, causing them to sputter and steam. Other sailors held back, afraid of the great beast.

A black feathered crossbow bolt thunked into the deck near Kormak and stood there quivering. Another ripped the night air over his shoulder. Panicked crossbowmen fired at the snake.

A couple of bolts quivered in the coils of the scaly horror. The ghost snake struck, head arcing down towards Kormak. Ignoring the bolts all around him, he lashed out with his blade, severing the creature's head. Cold blood fountained, splashing the furled sails. Coils exploded outwards and ripped through the air like a gigantic whip, knocking men flying, smashing into more lanterns, creating mayhem and chaos.

More oil splashed everywhere. The flames spread. Men kept firing their crossbows at the serpent, unaware that the thing was dead. Some of them hit their target in the tricky light. Others hit their companions.

Zamara still shouted orders, striding forward himself with a bucket of water and splashing it into the flames. A big bosun leapt in and started beating on the fire with a sailcloth.

As the snake ceased to writhe, the soldiers and crew fought down their panic and began to bring the fire under control. In the moonlight shining through the trees, Kormak caught sight of shadowy figures watching them from the undergrowth. They withdrew into the darkness, as if aware they had been spotted and unwilling to be seen.

**

"It was most likely pure chance," said Kormak, glancing at the forest. "The snake was disturbed by our passage, dropped onto the deck and killed the sailor by pure instinct."

Frater Jonas looked out over the guard-rail into the gloom under the trees. "They say the elves of the forest can control its beasts."

There was still a smell of burning in the air even though all the fires had been put out. Wounded men lay stretched out on blood-stained blankets, groaning despite the grog they had drunk to dull the pain. No one wanted to sleep. Everyone looked nervous.

"You think they put the snake up to attacking us?" Kormak said.

"They were out there, watching, I saw them. The elves have no reason to love men and many reasons to hate us."

"If they wanted us dead, they could have attacked from the riverbank while we were distracted by the fire and the serpent. Elves are deadly shots."

Jonas nodded. "It is not the only possibility. Perhaps the Kraken too can control such beasts. There are spells that would let him do it."

"How would he even know we are here? He does not know we are hunting him?"

The priest tilted his head to one side like a bird considering a worm. "There are spells of divination that could reveal our presence. And those are not the only methods of finding things out. Many folk in Siderea sell secrets for a share of pirate spoils. It is possible that our prey is forewarned of our presence."

Kormak's own instincts were also to think the worst in situations like this. "We had best be prepared for more attacks."

"I have mentioned the possibility to our captain. He may not like me but he understands reason when it is presented to him."

The priest stood silent for a moment, glanced at the wounded. "I do not like this place," he said. "I do not like being here. I do not like the sense that something terrible could happen at any moment."

"It's not like being back in the palace, is it?" Kormak said.

The priest laughed. "On the contrary, it is very similar. Both are treacherous environments, full of danger."

Kormak found himself smiling. Frater Jonas kept talking. His voice was quiet and reflective. "I grew up in a small village on the great plateau. My parents kept a wine shop and their own small fields. It was too cold in winter, too hot in summer but I loved the place. Life was simple. I sometimes wish I had stayed there."

"Why didn't you?"

"I was good with my letters, quick, sharp - the local priest saw possibilities in me. I was sent to one of the Order of the Sun's schools. I was educated, trained, dispatched on the Order's business, eventually I found my way to court. Your own life must have been very similar."

"Yes," Kormak said. He was wary. He had known other men who exchanged small confidences in the hopes of gaining larger ones. The priest looked thoughtful and sincere, but there were many who had that gift. If Jonas noticed his sudden reticence he gave no sign.

"An Aquilean in the Order of the Dawn—I thought you hill-men were all heathens."

Kormak very much doubted that. Jonas was an educated man. He was also no doubt familiar with the technique of saying something provocative just to get a response. "Some are believers. Some are not."

"Much the same as anywhere else then," said Jonas. "How did you come to join your Order?"

The question hung there in the air. Kormak considered for a moment and said, "My village was wiped out by an Old One when I was a child. I was the only survivor. The Guardian hunting the killer took me back to Mount Aethelas."

Frater Jonas looked a little embarrassed. "I am sorry. I was merely curious."

"It was all a long time ago."

"Did the Guardian ever catch the Old One?"

"No. The creature is still out there. He said he would come back for me one day. He has done such things before."

"Is that why the Order trained you?"

"Perhaps. Or perhaps they simply saw the potential in me, as your Order saw the potential in you."

"I have heard it said you are the greatest swordsman of this age of the world."

"I have known better."

"And yet you are still here."

"I did not say I fought them."

The priest laughed. "Then you are clever as well as good with a blade."

"It is a prerequisite for my work. Yours too, I suspect."

"Has the captain been telling you I am a spy?"

"Yes."

"He's not wrong."

"I am surprised you admit it."

"You already know it to be true. There is little point in denying it."

"So why are you here?"

The priest remained silent for a long time. He seemed to be considering his words very carefully or perhaps debating whether he should speak at all. "The Kraken is a most unusual man."

"How so?"

"You were right earlier. Most sorcerers don't become pirates—they prefer less active lives."

"Some have almost taken my head off with a blade."

Father Jonas shrugged. "He leads ships against our treasure fleets, against our merchants, against our colonies."

"Our?"

"Siderea's. King-Emperor Aemon's."

"He has a dislike for Sidereans."

"Indeed. And for our king in particular."

There was a stillness in the priest's manner now. He was watching Kormak very carefully. "A personal resentment?"

Jonas glanced over his shoulder to make sure no one was within earshot. "You could say that—he's King Aemon's brother."

"You're telling me Prince Taran has a secret life as a bloodthirsty pirate?"

"No. Prince Taran is, as he always has been, the king's strong right arm. The Kraken is more in the nature of a half-brother."

"I see."

"In his youth the last king, Varlan, Aemon's father, at that time Prince Varlan, had a brief, unfortunate affair with a woman from the Pirate Islands. Her name was Naomi. She was lovely, enchantingly lovely - *too* enchantingly lovely, it turned out. The prince was mad for her and some suspected it was because of more than her beauty. She was a sorceress and she was with child by the soon-to-be king. Varlan was already engaged to Lady Elanor who was and is a most jealous woman. Assassins were sent to slay Naomi and remove a potential embarrassment but they met a horrible death. The inquisition sought her out, but she vanished. No one thought any more of it and for a long time there was no need to, then the Kraken appeared in Port Blood. He claimed to be the rightful ruler of Siderea. It turned out his mother's name was Naomi. By all accounts he could be the twin of our king."

"It takes more than the royal blood to become king. The nobles must be behind you. You need an army. You need wealth."

"You know that. I know that. A madman raised by a resentful, ambitious witch might not or might not care. Particularly not a madman with a considerable gift for sorcery. It runs in the royal blood-line you know."

"The blood of Emperors," Kormak said. The kings of Siderea claimed descent from the ancient Solari mage-kings.

"Indeed," said Jonas.

"A wizard who is fighting his own private war with the Siderean crown... that's not something I have encountered before."

"Life is full of little surprises, isn't it? That's what keeps it interesting."

"You've tried to have him killed, of course."

The priest looked rueful. "Of course. Assassins have no more luck against him than against his mother."

"Why does he risk himself on these raids when he must know your king seeks his death?"

"He is overconfident, or perhaps merely justifiably confident, who am I to say? And he is looking for something."

Kormak sensed the tension in the priest. They were coming to the crux of the matter. "How do you know?"

"The ships he attacked, the places he raided, the mansions he burned, all had something in common. The ships were carrying artefacts from the Sunken Kingdoms. The mansions belonged to collectors of such artefacts, or held the libraries of scholars who specialised in such things."

"What kind of artefacts?"

"All of them were connected with the Quan." His voice was barely a whisper. Sailors still feared the Quan. They were mentioned in horrific legends in every port in the world.

"The servants of Dhagoth? The sea demons? "

"The same." Kormak considered this. The Old One Dhagoth had ruled large sections of the ocean when the world was young. He had been a rival of Saa-Aquor, the patron of merfolk. The Quan were deep sea dwellers. They had been mighty sorcerers, soul eaters. They were thought extinct, vanished along with their master during the wars of the Age of Darkness, leaving only legends that still terrified strong men. He doubted anyone collected their relics with a good purpose in mind.

"The Merchant's Guild did not hire me, did it?"

Frater Jonas shook his head. "The donation to your Order was made in their name but ultimately the money comes from the royal purse."

"The merchants are loyal supporters of the crown."

"Precisely so."

"You waited a long time to tell me this."

"I've told you now. When you needed to know it."

"And when there's not much chance of me being able to tell

anybody else."

"Your understanding of the situation is very sound. And I trust I have no need to add that everything I have told you is considered a state secret and that you should keep it in strictest confidence."

"King Aemon really wants the Kraken dead, doesn't he?"

"It's why you are here."

"I am not sure I like being used as an assassin."

"You've done it before. And if you do it this time, you won't find the King-Emperor ungrateful. Like all kings Aemon is wary of rivals, particularly ones who are potent mages. The man who rids him of this one could expect a considerable display of gratitude."

"Which is why *you* are here. To make sure everything goes smoothly, to report back on what happens."

The priest opened his hands. "I am merely a servant of my Order."

"One who may end up with a palace of his own." Kormak considered for a moment. "Or head of his Order with the king's support."

"If the Holy Sun provides such a thing, I would be an ingrate to turn it down." They stood together in silence while Kormak considered his words.

"I had always heard that King Aemon was the next best thing to a saint," Kormak said. "That he spends all his time building temples and cathedrals and collecting holy relics when he is not healing the sick. You make him sound less than saintly."

"There have been many types of saint, Sir Kormak, some more worldly than others. It is not for me to judge the king."

"Nor for me either you imply."

Jonas shrugged. "There's one more thing, Sir Kormak."

"And what would that be?"

"King Varlan was unwise enough to give Naomi a token of his affections, a very special one which ensured that the guards would allow her into the palace. It was a ruby seal ring, one that had belonged to Varlan's grandmother. It seems the Kraken wears it now."

Kormak kept his expression neutral. It was an unwise gift. People would remember that ring and recognise it. It would bolster the Kraken's claim to be of royal blood. "The king wants this token of his sire's misplaced affections returned.

"It would be considered a great favour and, since the Kraken would not give it up while still living, proof of success in your mission."

"You've given me plenty to think about, Frater."

"Then once more I bid you good night," said Frater Jonas. "Let us hope nothing else disturbs our rest."

CHAPTER FOUR

NEXT MORNING THEY kept rowing upriver. The forest grew denser and the river narrower. Its waters were a muddy brown. The branches of the trees formed a great arch overhead, cutting out the sun.

Shadowy figures kept pace with them, weaving amid the boles of the trees. The branches overhead moved as if animals were scampering through them. Sometimes Kormak saw faces looking down at them. He pointed this out to Zamara.

"As long as they don't attack us, they are not a problem," the captain said. "They are probably just watching us to make sure we do no harm as we pass through their territory. If they were going to ambush us, they would have done so by now."

"Or they are waiting for something," Kormak said, looking out from the sterncastle. Nothing was visible in the woods. The drummer kept up the beat, the oars rose and fell, the warship moved against the current like a water bug on the surface of a pond.

"What would they be waiting for?"

Kormak remembered the Great Trees and the elves that served them. In the past he had spoken with those alien beings but he did not like to guess as to their motives or plans. "I don't know," he said.

***

The day passed. The wounded lay contemplating their bloodied limbs and making coarse jokes at the expense of the comrades who had shot them. The sailors went about the business of the ship. Frater Jonas sat on a bench and studied the text of The Book of the Sun as if he expected a visitation of Angels to come test him on his knowledge of scripture. Zamara dozed in his chair on the command deck, preserving his strength in case another crisis came upon them in the night. Terves stood at his shoulder watching him with the patience of an old family retainer.

The river snaked through the forest, and they travelled on hour after hour, through an unbreaking monotony of green. Now and again a sentinel bellowed a warning but by the time all eyes had focused, the elves, if elves they were, had gone.

In the early evening, another shout rang out. A canoe emerged from beyond an island in the river, moving down river towards the ship. On the prow stood a tall elf, arms wide and fingers outstretched so that they could see he had no weapon.

The crossbowmen fitted quarrels into their arbalests. Zamara hunched down as he made his way to the prow. It was a poor risk to expose himself to the arrows of an enemy. He was the commander.

"Greetings, men of the Sun," said the elves in unison. They spoke Solari well but in an antique form.

"Greetings," said Zamara. "What would you have of us?"

"I bring word for one aboard your ship. I would speak with him alone."

"Who among my crew has had dealings with the elves?"

"The Treekiller."

Kormak showed himself and the elves' heads all swivelled to look at him. They performed the act with an eerie precision, as if a single mind coordinated their actions.

"What would you speak of?" Kormak said.

"Matters not for the ears of your companions."

Zamara looked at him. "It might be a trap. How could they have known you were aboard? And why do they call you Treekiller? It does not sound like the name they would give a friend."

"It is a long story," Kormak said.

"Join me on the island, Treekiller, and we will have words, you and I."

"I'll talk with them," Kormak said. "We may as well know what they want."

"Very well, but I'll have my men cover you. If there's a problem dive into the water and swim for it."

Kormak looked at the half dozen elves. "If there's a problem I will kill them myself."

***

Kormak stepped out of the small boat and walked down the beach to reach the elves. They were tall and slender with fine ash-blonde hair, swept back to reveal pointed ears. They looked as alike as identical twins. The similarity was much greater than anything he had seen among other elvish nations.

"Gilean of Kayoga sends greetings," said one elf.

"And I greet her back. To whom do I speak?"

"I am Ralan. I speak for Tumitha. We are her children."

Kormak bowed his head. "What does the Great Tree wish of me?"

"She wishes to understand what you are doing here. Do you pursue someone?"

"A man from the sea, a sorcerer. He came this way on a ship not unlike my own."

The elves nodded in unison. "We know this man. He passed through our lands. He had that with him which caused Tumitha unease."

"What would that be?"

"A creature not even close to being a man. It was of a race unseen in these parts for five thousand winters."

"One of the Quan?"

"That is how they are known among your people. To the Triturids, they were known only as the Enemy."

The Triturids were another Elder Race, servants of the Old One Tritureon, who had dwelled along the coasts of the World Ocean many millennia ago. Their ruins could be found from the island of Thuria in the far north to the coasts of Solarea at the Gates of the Dragon Sea. "How do you know what the Triturids thought?"

"Tumitha gave them shelter. They lived under the shadow of her leaves for many summers. They fought against Dhagoth and his servants during the wars of the Eldrim. You are approaching Triturek, the greatest of their citadels. The sorcerer you seek is already within its walls. His presence has driven the Triturids into a frenzy."

"He has not passed beyond?"

"We would know if he had."

"I must find him then."

"Be careful in that place. Our people shun the city. It is tainted by the Shadow. It has seeped into the very stones of the place and warped all who live near. The Triturids are degenerate shadows of what they once were. Whatever this sorcerer and his Quan ally seek, it cannot be a good thing. Tumitha wishes you to know this."

"Why does she help me?"

"You freed her brother from the Shadow, even if you killed him. There is a debt there. And she bears no love for the Quan. Wicked they were in ancient times, and dark and fell and mighty. She doubts the passage of time has improved their nature."

"I had thought the Quan gone from this world along with their patron."

"So had she. She believed they died when their mother, the sea monster Leviathan was slain. This disturbs her. Perhaps one of the forgotten Powers of ancient days stirs."

Kormak wondered what else the Great Tree knew that it was not telling him. He felt enmeshed in a vast web. Father Jonas and his Order had own agenda. The Great Tree had its. Doubtless the Kraken and his inhuman ally had theirs.

"I thank you and I thank Tumitha," he said.

"Best be wary within Triturek. It is a vile place." Without saying anything more, the elves rose in unison and left. They did not look back.

***

"What did they want?" Zamara asked as Kormak clambered up the rope netting on the side of the ship and over the railing.

"They told me where the Kraken is."

"Where?"

"Less than a day away, in the ruins left behind by one of the Elder Races."

Father Jonas looked at him. A sour expression twisted his mouth, as if he had just bitten into bad fruit. "Do these ruins belong to the Quan?"

Kormak shook his head. "Their enemies, the Triturids."

The captain looked at them both, as if wondering what they were talking about.

"That does not make any sense," Jonas said. He frowned, black eyebrows joining together over his nose.

"The elves said another thing—the Kraken has a Quan with him."

"The Black Priest?" Jonas said.

"I believe so."

"That is not good news—the sage Petroneus claimed that the Quan were deadly sorcerers."

"They are also supposed to be extinct," said Kormak.

Jonas nodded. "In recent times there have been rumours out of Port Blood concerning their reappearance. One of our agents even connected them with the Kraken but my superiors dismissed the idea. They thought it was just someone who had heard of the Kraken's interest in elder world artefacts and jumped to a fanciful conclusion. It seems they were wrong."

"The Kraken is looking for something in the ruins, obviously, but what?"

"We don't need to know that," said Zamara. "All we need to do is stop him getting it."

"It would help if we knew what it was," said Jonas. "It might save us from any more unpleasant surprises."

"Join me in my cabin," said Zamara. "It is obvious there are things we need to talk about."

***

On a war-galley like the Ocean's Blade, even the captain's cabin was tiny with room for little more than a bed. It was little more than a sheet of wood dangling from chains that lay atop a large sea chest. Zamara took a seat on it and indicated they should sit at his small table.

Bolts fixed two chairs to the floor near it.

"Tell me about these Quan," he said. "Now!"

Jonas looked at Kormak and then back at the captain. "They are an Elder Race long thought vanished from the world."

"Not any more if Sir Kormak's pointy-eared friends are to be believed."

"The elves have no reason to lie," said Kormak. "At least not about that."

Jonas looked at them as a teacher might consider two bickering students. He cleared his throat and said, "In the Age of Shadow, the Quan dwelled beneath the waves of the World Sea worshipping the Old One Dhagoth, the rider of Leviathan, Lord of the Darkest Depths. They were his greatest servants, mighty sorcerers. They consumed the souls of their victims. When Dhagoth warred with his greatest enemy Tritureon, they were his army. The two Old Ones fought a terrible war for control of the sea and destroyed each other. The sages believed their servants all perished with them."

"It seems some survived," said Zamara.

"We do not know much about the Servitor Races like the Quan and the Triturids," Frater Jonas said. "Some of them are believed to be immortal. Some could lie seemingly dead for centuries, perhaps millennia, before returning to life."

Kormak thought of some of the creatures he had encountered in his own life and about what Tumitha's mouthpiece had said about the Quan. He nodded.

A knock sounded against the door. "We have found ruins, sir," Terves reported. "You had better see them for yourself."

Zamara let out a long sigh. "I believe it is time to return to the command deck," he said.

***

The crew and soldiers fell silent as they rowed under the shadow of the great walls. Massive carved stone heads resembling those of gigantic frogs looked down on them. Kormak wondered if they represented the children of Tritureon, created by him from his own blood if the ancient legends were to be believed.

"It is a city of demons," one of the soldiers said.

Frater Jonas looked on wide-eyed and made the Sign of the Sun over his heart.

The wall was perhaps fifty feet high and perhaps thirty feet thick, built from massive stone blocks fitted together and then fused by sorcery. Along the edges where they met it looked like the stone had melted and run together. Lichen covered all of the blocks and all of the demon heads.

A stink of rot filled the air. He had come to associate that stench with Shadowblights. He pulled the wraithstone amulet from beneath his armour and inspected it. Was there just the faintest dark taint in its centre? It was hard to spot. The amulet was a new one he had picked up on his way to Trefal. There were no traces of exposure to the Shadow just yet, but there would be soon if he entered this place.

They rowed until ahead of them they saw a trireme tied up at a long stone pylon. Zamara gave the order to prepare for battle and all eyes were on the strange vessel as they approached. There was no sign of life on it. No crew were visible.

"What is going on?" Zamara asked, clearly frustrated to find no enemy. Kormak fingered the hilt of his own dwarf-forged blade. He suspected a trap.

"Don't get too close," he said. Zamara looked at him as if to say he would not dream of doing so.

"We could sink it from here," he said. "There's nothing to stop us."

"Please do not do that, captain," Frater Jonas. "At least not until the Guardian and I have had a chance to investigate."

"There might be a score of pirates hiding below deck right now," Zamara said. "The Black Priest might be there working sorcery to destroy us."

"Then best keep your distance. Give me half a dozen marines and I will go aboard and see what I can find." Frater Jonas looked at Kormak. "I assume you will wish to come with me."

"I would not miss the opportunity for the world," said Kormak, unable to keep the irony from his voice.

CHAPTER FIVE

THE OARSMEN BROUGHT the small rowboat closer to the pirate vessel. The only sounds were the splash of the oars in the water, the creaking of the ship ahead of them. No one spoke. The crew kept their eyes fixed on the pirate vessel as if they expected someone to pop up at any moment and start taking shots at them.

Spears jutted from the pirate vessel's sides. Their serrated blades looked carved from the same stone as the city walls.

In the water a man floated, face down. He was garbed in a yellowish shirt with a ruffled collar. His hair was red. His beard curled. Something short and sharp protruded from his neck. More corpses floated in the brackish water close to the ship.

"Well, we know what happened to some of the Kraken's men," Kormak said.

"Tossed over the side, most likely. A pirate burial," said Terves.

Kormak swarmed up the netting and vaulted over the railing. Ropes lay coiled on the decks, unlit lanterns swung from the masts.

More sharp objects protruded from the carved wood of the railing. He pulled a needle-sharp sliver of stone free. A smudge of bitter smelling paste clung to the tip. A poison, no doubt.

He stalked across the deck, every nerve stretched taut. Scores of darts protruded from the planking. He pictured a cloud of them arcing downward from the walls above the dock.

Had the Kraken and his men been ambushed by the inhabitants of the city and carried off? That would explain the silence on the ship.

He moved to the stairs beneath the sterncastle and looked down. No one hid there. He studied the benches of the open deck. There were no chains so it looked as if the oarsmen were all volunteers, which did not surprise him. Pirates fought for a share of the spoils and most successful captains could have their pick of crews.

He stopped and listened. Still no sounds save those he would have expected on an abandoned ship. He moved back to the rail and gestured for Frater Jonas and the marines to come aboard.

The priest came over the side, out of breath, his cheeks flushed and red.

"What happened here?" Jonas asked.

"A battle between the pirates and the locals. They tossed the bodies overboard but left too quickly to clear away all the signs of battle."

Frater Jonas walked over to the stairs beneath the sterncastle, and asked, "Is it clear?"

"I have not been below the sterncastle, but I have heard nothing."

The priest made an elaborate bow. A sweep of his arm indicated that Kormak was welcome to precede him. The Guardian gave a sour grin and made his way down the stairs. They did not creak beneath his weight. He tested them before putting his full weight on them.

He paused at the foot of the stairs to give his eyes time to accustom themselves to the gloom. A strange scent hung in the air, a salt sea tang mingled with the stench of corruption. It reminded him of the fishermen's wharves of Trefal on a hot summer day after a cargo of spoiled cod had been dropped ashore.

The stairs creaked as Frater Jonas came down. His hand held his Elder Sign. His lips silently mouthed prayers. His glance darted everywhere as if he expected an attack. Kormak pushed on down the corridor.

The ceiling was so low he had to crouch. Openings to left and right led to tiny cabins. One door to the back of the ship opened onto the cabin space sacred to a captain's privacy. Kormak tried the door of it and found it unlocked.

The cabin was bigger than he would have expected and the smell of rot and fish was stronger. Greenish residue coated the walls in places, as if something slimy had been dragged along them and then dried. It glowed in the gloom, like the scum that Kormak had seen at night on certain haunted beaches.

Beside the sleeping bench stood a table. On it lay an unrolled map held down by brass paperweights. It showed a large hexagon surrounded by a green expanse with a blue ribbon running down one side. Inside the hexagon were numerous smaller ones all bordered in blue. Most of the shapes were green in colour but some were also filled in with blue. At the centre was a much larger hexagon, many, many times the size of the smaller ones. This had been marked in ink with a red runic cross.

"What does it mean?" Kormak asked.

"It's a map," said Jonas. "I am guessing of Triturek." He ran a finger down the blue ribbon. "Look, that's the river, see the way it curves?" He traced the huge hexagon that filled the map. "Those are the external walls. The green is the forest."

Kormak nodded. It was simple when pointed out. He had been

looking for sorcerous runes or Elder Signs, not a simple chart.

"I guess we'll find out what the rest is when we go into the city."

Beneath the bunk was a sealed chest with a sorcerous lock, the kind that could only be opened by the touch of the mage who had cast the spell. Kormak withdrew the Elder Sign from beneath his armour and pressed it against the lock. The sigil grew warm as it disrupted the spell then, after a moment, began to cool.

"That was not the wisest of things," said Frater Jonas. "There might have been a trap, or it may be poisoned or there may be something within."

"What's done is done."

"Quite," said the priest. Kormak dragged the chest out from beneath the bunk, stood to one side and then opened the lid with the point of his dagger.

Within lay a dozen charts and scrolls and books. Frater Jonas scanned them. He nodded as he read, as if what he saw confirmed something.

"Grimoires?" Kormak asked. He could see the crabbed notation on the pages as Jonas read. Each held the small script and cryptic diagrams he had come to associate with the journals of sorcerers.

Jonas nodded with the excitement of a scholar who has come unexpectedly on a treasure trove. He put one book on the bed and lifted another, flipped through its pages then repeated the process. He unrolled one of the charts. His eyes narrowed and a frown of puzzlement creased his brow. He glanced at another and then yet at a book. He leafed through it, put it aside.

"There is a king's ransom in spellcraft here," he said. Jonas inspected a few more of the books and scrolls before wrapping them in a blanket that smelled of rotten fish. He used it as a bag to carry his plunder.

"What did you get?"

"We've found some of the grimoires the Kraken stole," he said. "He's made notes on them. There's a book written in gibberish, which I am assuming is a coded journal."

"And the charts that so puzzled you."

Jonas shrugged. "They are maps but of what I do not know. One of them was a chart showing the location of this city. It was marked with runes I have never seen before in a language I have never read."

Next to the Kraken's cabin lay another small room. Half a dozen desiccated, long-dead looking corpses hung manacled to its walls. Most of them wore the homespun tunics and britches of villagers. One of them was robed in yellow and white, a preacher.

"Those were the prisoners from Wood's Edge," Kormak said.

"Yes," said Frater Jonas. He looked ill. "They weren't prisoners though—they were food."

Kormak nodded. "The Quan devoured them."

"It must have used a lot of energy when it cast those spells back in the village. It needed replenishment."

"Perhaps," Kormak said.

"Perhaps?"

"Perhaps it saved some of the prisoners till now, to power its magic here in the city. Why else bring them?"

Jonas considered for a moment, his eyes wide and haunted-looking. "Yes," he said. "You are most likely correct."

"A dangerous creature to have on board," Kormak said. "If it gets hungry it might decide to feed on the crew."

"What sort of man would make pacts with demons like these?" Jonas asked.

"I would rather know what it is they are seeking," Kormak said. He already knew the sort of man the Kraken was, one so ambitious he dealt with anything that had the power to gratify his desires.

"I fear we will both know that before this thing ends," said Jonas.

"Come, we'd best tell the captain what we found."

***

"A fishy smell?" Zamara wrinkled his nose and looked at them in disbelief. Once more they crowded into his small cabin. "What do you mean?"

"Unless the Kraken has decided that he likes to eat lots of rotten herring, it means his companion is not human," Kormak said.

"It must be a Quan," said Frater Jonas.

Zamara looked at them. "I don't care if it is a manifestation of the Shadow itself. We need to find the Kraken and bring him to justice."

"No one disagrees, captain," said Jonas. "We need to be aware of the nature of our potential foes though."

"What now?" Zamara was frustrated. The captain was a man of action and he had nerved himself for a fight. The fact there was no battle was worse for him than a call to arms.

"We need to find out what happened to the Kraken. The elves were sure he's somewhere in the city and that he's going to be until he finds whatever it is he is looking for. Then he's going to have to come back for his ship if he wants to escape." Frater Jonas sounded distracted. He was busy transferring the books and scrolls from the blanket to a waterproof leather satchel.

"Do you think you can find anything useful from those stinking books you brought back?" Zamara demanded. "Or do you just plan on selling them to the highest bidder."

Frater Jonas looked hurt. "If they are sold, you and the crew will get your share," Jonas said. "If. Right now they are the only clue we have as to what this pirate-sorcerer is up to."

"Very well," said Zamara. "We'll put a prize crew on the pirate ship. Leave a guard here and head into the city with the rest of the troops. You can stay or go as you please. Sir Kormak should come with us. If we meet the Kraken and his black-cowled friend I want him there with his blade."

Kormak did not like his tone but what he said was sensible.

"I'll come with you," said Frater Jonas. "I am rather curious about this city."

CHAPTER SIX

"THAT'S THE PLACE marked on the map," said Frater Jonas, pointing at the enormous ziggurat. They had entered the city through the great hexagonal gate near the docks. The priest had brought the satchel along and stood consulting the map of the city now.

An eerie assemblage of low windowless stone buildings lay between stagnant canals. He sniffed the air. It smelled of scum and stagnant water.

All of the low buildings stood on hexagonal islands, isolated by canals. Around each ran narrow walkways like canal towpaths. Arched stone bridges joined the islands. Ramps rose from the paths to the roofs of some of the buildings.

The structures looked eroded by time and damp. The stonework had crumbled in places, leaving the sides of some of the buildings looking like rotten teeth in an ancient beggar's mouth. Moss grew on everything and vines dangled from walls. From the centre of some buildings enormous banyan-like trees raised their branches to the sky. Their roots sought the water like the tentacles of a great beast.

"Looks like this place was abandoned a long time ago," said Zamara.

"It looks like all the inhabitants died of plague," said Frater Jonas. He made the Sign of the Sun over his breast.

"That's not what the elves said," said Kormak. "They say the original inhabitants are still here. They are the survivors of the war between Dhagoth and Tritureon."

Zamara shrugged, as if to say he did not really care what the forest dwellers thought. "It does not look like they've kept their homes in good repair then."

"How would we know what good repair means to them," said Kormak. He agreed with Zamara but he did not like the captain's sneering tone. The more nervous the captain was, the more arrogant his manner became.

"We'd best be going if we are going to find the Kraken and claim the bounty," said Zamara.

He spoke loudly for the benefit of the marines. The warriors eyed the buildings as if at any moment they expected a horde of Old Ones to erupt from them.

"That's a bloody big pyramid," said Terves. "It's as big as the king's palace back in Trefal. Bigger maybe."

There was a note of awe in his voice. He was thinking about the beings who could build such an enormous structure. It must smack of magic in his mind. Even in its ruined state the city was far larger than any a Siderean soldier was likely to have seen and it was certainly much stranger.

The line of soldiers straggled along the narrow walkways at the water's edge. There were no doorways in the side of the buildings. Gurgling noises told Kormak that there might be entrances below the water level within the canals themselves. Carvings covered the sides of the buildings, demonic crested frog-like heads emitting water in fountains. Creepers covered the buildings. Trees grew through the paving stones here and there.

"What's this?" Zamara asked. He bent down over something. They looked like the prints of wet, webbed feet left on the stonework. Something about the distance between the prints told Kormak they had not been left by anything that walked like a man.

"I don't know," Kormak said. "Tracks of something."

"The Triturids had webbed feet," Frater Jonas said. "So the legends say."

"Then where are they?" the captain asked. It was a good question. The tracks came from the water's edge, moved along the path and then vanished again, as if whatever had made them had leapt back into the water.

"If we wait here long enough we might find out," Kormak said. "But our business is elsewhere."

Zamara gestured for the troops to move on. Kormak felt as if something was looking at him but he was not sure from where. A cloud of bubbles disturbed the stagnant water of the canal. He stared at it for a long time but nothing emerged.

Buzzing clouds of insects filled the air. They were large as hummingbirds and their forms were distorted. Their wings glistened with oily colours, catching the sun's light and reflecting it. Huge pad-like flowers floated in the water, along with masses of congealed algae. Heavy splashes sounded in the distance. The water surface rippled. Not once did they see any sign of what had caused the disturbance.

A crawling sensation erupted between Kormak's shoulder blades. He knew he was being watched by something malignant, yet no matter which way he turned or how quickly he did so, he could find no sign of any stalker.

All around he heard stealthy sounds; splashes, the ripple of water, the whistle of wind. It was as if the city was slowly, almost imperceptibly mobilising against them.

The marines remained silent as they walked, crossbows at the ready, swords loose in their scabbards. Captain Zamara stood in their midst, ready to give orders. Kormak led the way, flanked by Frater Jonas who seemed to feel safest when he was in closest proximity to the Guardian.

"I can see why the elves told you to avoid this place," Jonas said. He tilted his head to one side and contemplated the scummy water. "It stinks of the Shadow. There are signs of blight everywhere."

"There are," said Kormak. He pulled out the wraithstone amulet again. The white surface was notably darker. "If we stay here more than a few days it will start to affect us."

Jonas nodded. He had already told the troops the same things that Kormak would have—drink no water collected within the city, eat nothing they found there. Not that there was much danger of the latter. Nothing they had seen since entering the city looked appetising. He could not imagine even the hungriest man wanting to eat anything they found here.

"How old do you think this place is?" Zamara asked. He studied the buildings all around them. Some looked like they could have been built yesterday. Some looked like they had crumbled centuries ago. Some looked like they had been burned by a fire so hot that the stone had flowed like lava before resetting. There was no rhyme or reason to it.

Frater Jonas stroked his beard and said, "Such records as I have seen date the Triturids' occupation of these coasts back to deep within the Age of Darkness. More than ten thousand years ago."

Zamara frowned. "Those elves told you that their mistress, this Great Tree God of theirs gave shelter to them. Does that mean she remembers all the way back in time?"

Kormak remembered his encounter with ghost of Mayasha. "Yes," he said. "They are as old as the forests and they remember everything, just not in the way we do."

"Then this place must predate the Kingdoms of the Sun by at least five thousand years," the captain said.

"At least," said Frater Jonas. "Perhaps by a lot more. They say the Old Ones walked these lands for tens of thousands of years before the coming of men, and many of them were accompanied by their children."

"They ruled the world once, didn't they? Before the coming of the Holy Sun." Zamara said.

"They did," said the priest, clearly uncomfortable with the way this conversation was drifting.

The captain glanced at the great pyramid, then at the ruins, then at Kormak. "What were they?"

"No one knows," Kormak said.

"You have met them though, haven't you? You've fought with them, talked with them? What are they like?"

All around there was silence. Every man within earshot was listening. Even Father Jonas looked expectant. Kormak thought of the scores of Old Ones he had encountered in his life, the still living and the now dead, the hostile and the almost friendly and the totally alien. What could he say about so many and so varied creatures?

"They did not tell me their secrets," he said.

His tone put an end to the questioning.

***

Kormak strode up the ramp onto the roof of one of the buildings. A sunken pool lay before him. The place was dry save for puddles of stagnant rainwater now. In the centre a shaft dropped. He clambered down and looked in. Far below, dark water rippled.

He could see other buildings, mostly of the same height and uniform construction. Pools of water glittered on some of their roofs, evidence perhaps that their ancient hydraulic systems still worked.

Even from this low elevation, the hexagonal nature of the islands was evident. The pattern was the same as on the map they had found in the Kraken's cabin.

A light glittered on the side of the great ziggurat, as if a weapon or a shield or a polished mirror caught the sunlight.

He headed back to ground level. Zamara looked at him. "All done?" he asked.

"I think we'll find what we're looking for at the central ziggurat," Kormak said. "I don't think we're alone in the city."

"Tell me something I didn't know," said the nobleman.

**

They picked their way along the canals, making for the great central ziggurat. The priest stared at one of the frog-mask faces as they passed.

"The Triturids were ugly devils," he said.

"They would probably have said the same about us," Kormak said.

"The Old Ones looked at things differently from us, didn't they?"

"Not all of them," Kormak said.

"The most powerful ones from the Age of Darkness certainly did. And now we walk in one of their strongholds. It is a rather frightening thought."

"You seem nervous, Frater."

"Unlike you, Sir Kormak, I have not spent most of my life in such places slaying monsters."

"And yet you are here. Why? You could have stayed with the ship."

"I am curious. There must be much knowledge to be gained here. I have never been in such a place before and the Light willing I will never be in such a place again but while I am here I would like to look upon it. How many opportunities like this does a man like myself get in one lifetime?" He sounded sincere but Kormak wondered if he had another motive.

A man ahead shrieked. Kormak raced to his side. "What is it?" he asked.

The marine looked pale. "I saw something."

"What?"

"A monster. A green-skinned monster." The captain had joined them. "What did it look like?"

"Like a monstrous lizard, but not like a lizard, like a man, and not like a man, like an insect..."

The soldier's voice broke. Zamara slapped his face with a cold precision. The man started, then clenched his fists. He straightened his back and pulled in his stomach. When he spoke again it was in the dispassionate tone of a warrior making a report to a superior. "It was green-skinned, somewhat man-like, sir. It had six limbs and it was moving on four of them. Its face was like that of a toad with a great crest that started on its head and seemed to run down its back. I caught sight of it from the corner of my eye and then it vanished into the canal."

The captain looked at Kormak and then the priest.

"It sounds like a Triturid," Jonas said.

"An Old One, sir?" the soldier asked.

"One of their spawn," Kormak said.

"It was watching us, sir. I think it left those prints we saw awhile back. Its feet were webbed and it sort of glistened, sir..."

"Glistened?"

"Like its skin was slick or slimy, like a fish's."

"Where did it go?"

"The canal, sir. At least I think so."

Jonas nodded. "That explains how they follow us without being seen. They're under the water."

"We're surrounded by canals," Zamara said. He looked worried.

"The Triturids use them like we use streets."

A soldier nearby gave a small shriek. Kormak turned to see him pointing at something. "Eyes, sir, eyes in the water."

Kormak turned and saw what the man was pointing at. Two huge orbs gazed up at him from the water. Before they might have been mistaken for a ripple, or just overlooked entirely but now that he knew what he was looking for, he saw them clearly. The eyes submerged and vanished.

"Well," said Zamara. "We definitely know we're not alone."

Kormak thought of the hexagonal pools he had seen on the building roofs. He thought about the possibility of underwater entrances and connecting tunnels. It would be easy for them to be ambushed if the natives proved hostile. And he did not doubt for a moment that they would.

CHAPTER SEVEN

A SCREAM RANG out. A man fell clutching at his neck, his face already green. Froth bubbled from his mouth. Kormak pulled a stone dart from the marine's neck. Traces of the poison paste smudged it. The man's body heaved. The veins bulged on his neck. Stillness settled on him. The rest of the soldiers backed away as if death might prove contagious.

Jonas stretched out his hand for the stone weapon and took it with the tips of his fingers. He held it the way a man might grip a poisonous reptile. Sweat glistened on his brow. Dark circles stained the armpits of his robe. He brought the point up to eye level and inspected it then moved it just under his nostrils and sniffed.

"Swamp snake venom," he said. "Kills in instants, stops the heart."

Kormak cocked his head to one side. Now did not seem to be a good time to ask the priest how he had come by his knowledge of esoteric poisons. He tried to judge the direction from which the weapon had come. It must have been fired from the canal. From one particular spot circles rippled out, as if someone had lobbed a stone into the water, or a large object had just submerged.

"Anybody see anything?" Kormak asked. "The attack came from

the water. Somebody must have noticed something."

The soldiers' shook their heads. Frater Jonas held the dart up between two fingers. "It's very light and very sharp," he said.

"Something still threw it and I doubt it was invisible," Kormak said.

Frater Jonas shook his head, a movement as small as a leaf quivering under the weight of an insect.

"We can't know that for sure," said Zamara, voicing the priest's silent fear. "We can't know anything about this accursed place."

From the expression on his face, he was sorry they had ever come here.

The ripples vanished, the dead man stared at the sky with forlorn eyes. Kormak sensed something out there, watching him.

"We could go back," said Zamara. He kept his voice low so that the soldiers would not hear. Most of them stood with their backs against the walls of the buildings while a few stood guard. One or two of their heads swivelled as if they heard their captain's words.

"We could," said Frater Jonas. "We could wait at the docks. The Kraken is not going anywhere without his ship."

"The docks might already have been attacked," said Kormak, voicing what nobody else seemed to want to. "The Kraken's ship was. Ours might be as well. And we know by what now."

"The Triturids," said Jonas.

"We've only seen one," said Zamara. "Hell, most of us have not even seen that."

"A lot more than one attacked the Kraken's ship judging by the number of spears sticking from its side," said Kormak.

"He probably just left a skeleton crew," said the nobleman. "We've left a lot more."

"It still might not be enough."

Zamara considered things for a moment and came to a decision. "We're here to find the Kraken and take his head and by the Light of the Holy Sun that is what we will do."

The priest nodded agreement. Both of them looked at Kormak. He shrugged. "If he's here, we'd best find him. Let's keep going to the central ziggurat."

"All right, men," the captain shouted. "On your feet. We're going for a little stroll."

Grumbling and nervous, the marines made ready to move off.

***

One moment they were marching along the canal side, the next a cloud of spears and darts descended on them.

Kormak's blade flashed from its scabbard and swept through the air, deflecting the missiles aimed at him, sending them clattering to the ground at his feet.

"On the roof," Zamara shouted. Crossbow men turned and fired. Kormak saw a row of green-skinned, six-limbed warriors arrayed against the skyline. They walked on their four rear limbs like beasts but in their front pair of arms, the ones protruding from their shoulders, they held stone spears and darts.

The Triturids raised long tubes to their lips. Their huge throats pulsed and their massive chests shrank, as if expelling every last breath of air in their lungs. A hail of missiles erupted from their blowpipes. A storm of darts rained down on the men. Kormak understood how they had struck from the river without being seen. Only the tube of the blowpipe broke the surface, hard to spot in the murky polluted water.

"Crossbowmen prepare to fire," the captain shouted. "Steady, you dogs! Wait for me to give the word."

Zamara stood tall, sword in hand, shouting orders, even as darts bearing terrible death clattered down all around him. A serrated edged spear pierced the chest of the man beside him and the captain did not break stride. He shouted, "Fire!"

A score of crossbow bolts scythed the air. A dozen of the Triturids fell. The rest ducked out of sight. A few corpses were visible with their webbed feet protruding over the edge. They slid from view, dragged by their companions.

Kormak scrambled up the corner of the building using the protruding statues, emerging onto the roof just in time to see the amphibians pulling their fallen companions into the pool. Trails of green blood and slime led all the way from the roof's edge to the water. Crossbow bolts lay on the stone where they had fallen.

The last of the Triturids turned to look at him. Standing upright on its spindly hind limbs, the amphibian would have been a head taller than he. A webbed crest rose from its skull. Its mottled skin glistened green, moist and slimy. Two massive eyes situated on either side of the head regarded him. A long, pink tongue whipped out and then back. Huge nostrils flared and shrank. As Kormak stepped towards it, the creature's chest inflated and its powerful limbs sent it hopping backwards into the pool. It splashed down and did not reappear.

He stalked to the edge of the pool. He saw nothing but his own reflection in the dark water and stepped back lest he become a target. His suspicions had proved correct. The pools and canals connected, providing a highway for the city's inhabitants. He stalked towards to the edge of the roof shouting, "Don't shoot! It's me, Kormak! I am coming down!"

Below him crossbowmen looked nervous but none of them pulled the trigger. Kormak sprang down.

"What did you find?" Jonas asked.

"Nothing," Kormak said. "They were all gone."

"Vanished into thin air?" The priest looked disbelieving.

"Into dark water," Kormak said and explained about the connecting pools.

"It's not going to get any easier," Zamara said.

***

The running battle became more intense the closer they got to the central ziggurat.

"They're fighting like elves," Kormak said, looking at the dead body of the Triturid at his feet. Splayed out, it was almost half as long again as a man. Its long thin limbs twitched. Even in death it seemed unable to keep still.

"Bastards," Zamara wiped the slimy green from his shirt and inspected his soldiers. Almost half of them were dead. Sometimes a man survived a poisoned dart, perhaps because of some natural immunity to the toxin or because of a diluted dosage. Mostly though, they died.

"They won't stand and fight. They attack and then they dive into their pools or canals and swim away. It is not honourable."

Frater Jonas's laughter was bitter. "But it is clever. They reduce their casualties and they increase ours. They slow our movement and they cost us precious time."

"You think they are in league with the Kraken?" Zamara asked.

Jonas shook his head. "I think they are protecting what is theirs. If I were a gambling man I would bet they were trying to prevent us going closer to the citadel. They only attack us on paths that turn towards it. Maybe they are sending a message."

"They could have just written us a letter," said Zamara. He laughed at his own joke. None of the others did. They were too tired or too afraid. It was nerve-wracking, waiting for a poison dart from an ambush, moving through a city filled with inhuman monsters.

Kormak counted the dead amphibians. There were less than half a dozen of them, most killed by crossbow bolts. The rest had hopped back into the water as the humans closed.

"They did not attack us at the dock," Kormak said. "They did attack the Kraken's ship."

"Maybe they followed him away," said Zamara.

"Or maybe they attacked his ship because they had reason to," said the priest.

"The Quan," said Kormak.

"The terrible thing here is we might be on the same side as these green-skinned bastards," said Zamara. "But we have no way of communicating that to them. How do you parlay with a bunch of giant six-limbed newts?"

"Just be grateful there are not more of them, or we would not be going anywhere except the funeral pyre," said Jonas.

Kormak studied the amphibian's corpse. In death its eyes were still open. Its tongue hung out. Its chest no longer pulsed and its limbs had stopped twitching. After the priest's words a twinge of sympathy entered his mind. The amphibians might be the savage, Shadow-tainted remnants of a once proud people but this was their home.

"Let's go," Zamara said. "The Holy Sun is not going to keep looking down on us forever."

***

The central ziggurat loomed ever larger, a six-sided mountain of damp greenish stone rising over the relative flatness of the city. Huge carved faces with bulging eyes and distended jaws spat fountains of water down its algae-covered sides. The steps of the pyramid jutted twice the height of a man, but ramps went up the side of the structure. Their curved sides were smooth. Going up them felt like crawling up a grain chute in a warehouse.

Kormak led the way. Behind him the men pulled themselves up the side of the ziggurat. He risked a glance back at the city.

The canals formed moats around blocks of buildings and flowed into large pools dominated by central hexagonal islands. The structures seemed the tips of gigantic towers emerging from an infinitely deep pool of semi-stagnant water.

The water shimmered black and vast. Sinister ripples moved across it, as if an enormous beast displaced it as it rose to the surface. He half-expected to see a massive head emerge.

After the sun's light died, a faint phosphorescent glow appeared on the surface of the water, giving the whole city a ghostly appearance.

He clambered on, knowing they did not have time now to return to the ship. They were going to have to make camp on top of the great six-sided pyramid. He wondered if they would survive the night.

CHAPTER EIGHT

PHOSPHORESCENT INSECTS SWARMED over the canals. Greenish balls of light drifted over the pools of murky water. Tendrils of mist rose like steam from a boiling pot, strange vapours produced by hidden things in the depths. The shadows of the buildings loomed out of the gloom. In the shimmer of moonlight and the stagnant waters' glow, Triturek had an eerie, inhuman beauty.

Kormak clambered over the lip of the chute and out onto the summit. He stood on a vast flat area of interlocked stone blocks. In the centre, the dark maw of a great pit loomed. The ashy remains of cooking fires spread across the flagstones.

The soldiers muttered and groaned as they emerged behind him. One of them helped Frater Jonas up. The priest breathed like a beached whale. Sweat soaked his robes.

Kormak walked over to the remains of another campfire. A broken grog bottle lay near it.

Zamara glanced at Jonas with something like contempt. He strode over to Kormak, looked down at the blackened stonework, knelt, stirred the ashes with a finger.

"The Kraken has been here," he said.

"He can't be too far ahead of us," Kormak said.

Zamara looked around and made an ironic sweep with his hand. "Unless he used the chutes to slide down the far side of this accursed pyramid."

"I suspect he went inside," Kormak said. He walked over to the gaping pit in the ziggurat's roof. Around its edges ran another ramp, smooth and flat and bounded by stonework carved with the faces of toad-headed demons. The ramp vanished down into the distance, turning at right angles at a new level below.

"The Triturids obviously did not believe in stairs," the captain said. He glanced over his shoulder. The soldiers had lined up on the edge of the ziggurat. One took a piss off its edge. Others watched the lights in the city below and whispered to each other. They seemed grateful to have reached a place where they could not be so easily ambushed. Frater Jonas sat down near the remains of the fire, letting his breathing subside.

"We're going to have to go in, aren't we?" He spoke softly so that the others could not hear.

"The Kraken came up here for a reason," Kormak said, "and I doubt it was simply to enjoy the fine views of the city. Whatever he is looking for is somewhere below us."

"We'll let the men get their breath back and then head down," Zamara said.

He paused for a while and then said, "Strange, strange place. I wonder what it was."

Frater Jonas picked himself and limped over. "I am guessing a temple."

Zamara walked over to the edge of the ziggurat. He tilted his head to one side, contemplating what he saw. "You could fit the port of

Trefal into a small corner of this city. What happened to it? Why was it abandoned?"

Jonas shrugged. "No one knows. I am curious about what is below."

"We all know what curiosity did to the cat," said the captain. He turned to the marines. "Break out the lanterns and torches, you sea-dogs. We're going below to find this bloody pirate and make him give an accounting for his crimes. And then we'll give a different sort of accounting to the Chancellor when we collect the bounty on the Kraken's head."

Tired as they were the men did not object. Kormak suspected they found the idea of facing pirates less intimidating than spending the night in the open atop the giant ziggurat.

✱✱

The torches flickered. The air stank of damp. Mould blotched the walls and ran like snot from the huge nostrils of the carved amphibian heads. The Elder Sign hanging against Kormak's chest was warming up. He glanced over the banister than ran down the side of the ramp. A long way below him lights glittered. The sound of distant dripping water rippled through the building.

More statues stood on hexagonal plinths. They resembled the Triturids, with enormous eyes and nostrils and long spindly limbs. Some of them carried multi-faceted gems, some of them brandished long spears tipped with serrated blades. Others carried blowpipes. All of them had great crested head-dresses attached to their brows. Long tongues protruded from some of their mouths.

The statues put the marines on edge. They made Elder Signs over their breasts and offered up prayers to the Sun. They believed they were looking at demons, and they might not have been far wrong.

The party emerged onto a landing.

Torchlight revealed flecks of colour on the wall, tiny glittering parts of a great mosaic, made from gems and glass. Terves pried a stone loose with his dagger. "Glass," he said in a tone somewhere between disgust and wonder.

Kormak inspected the mosaic. It depicted a towering six-limbed amphibian locked in conflict with a tentacled giant. Around their feet squid-faced humanoids battled a horde of Triturids in a number of settings; atop hexagonal ziggurats, in the churning waters of the sea, under the eaves of a great forest.

One mosaic depicted the tentacles of a gigantic monster erupting from the waves and smashing the walls of a city.

The images were all distorted, much broader and rounder than they should have been, as if produced by a being with sight that worked differently than a human's. Colours were subtly wrong although that might have been just the light.

"Gods at war," said Zamara, nodding at the mural.

"It must have been something like that," said Frater Jonas. "The Old Ones devastated kingdoms with their conflicts. They unleashed powers that twisted the world, that slew immortals, that laid waste to continents."

The monotonous drip, drip, drip continued. The air grew colder as it got moister. It was chilly in the depths of the pyramid in a way it had not been outside.

"What was this place?" Zamara asked. "The population of a small kingdom could live in here."

"Perhaps it has no function we would understand," Kormak said. "The Elder demons did not think like we do."

"This was the biggest structure in the city, it seems fair to assume it was a palace or a god's house," said Jonas. He was speaking just to disagree, to find an outlet for his nervousness. Kormak had seen men bicker this way before.

Something rippled and flowed a long way below, reflecting their lights and lights from elsewhere. A smell of rot filled the air. There was an oily taste on his tongue he had come to associate with the presence of blight.

Memories of the great pyramid of Forghast flooded back, a structure constructed to channel magical energy according to the principles of geomancy. Perhaps this place followed the same principles. The captain and the priest still debated.

"We need to get moving again," Kormak said. "If we are going to find the Kraken before he gets what he came here for."

***

They reached the bottom of the ramp. It disappeared into blackish, stagnant water that reflected the light of their torches like oil would.

Zamara ordered one of the soldiers he should go forward. Reluctantly the man walked down to the water's edge and began to wade forward. The liquid rose to his calves then his thighs then his waist as he walked but it did not seem to get any deeper. The man turned and returned to the company and stood, water dripping from his sodden britches.

"Cold," he said. "And scummy."

"We're going to have to go through it," said Kormak.

"But which way," the captain said.

Kormak glanced around. In the far distance, along a great tunnel-like corridor, lights could be seen. "That way looks as good as any other," he said.

***

The water sloshed by up to Kormak's waist. It dragged at his limbs, slowing his movements. It chilled his legs. The uneasy feeling that things were lurking below the oily surface niggled at his mind.

The currents tugged at his legs like tentacular monsters. He picked his way forward, fearing that there might be a great gaping hole in front of him.

A scream rang out and a man vanished. His torch hit the water's surface and extinguished with a hiss. Kormak moved towards him but a second later the soldier emerged from the water, liquid pouring from his hair and face. "Tripped," he said. He glared around as if fearing that in the time he had been under water, the rest of them might have disappeared.

A sloshing sound told Kormak that someone was at his shoulder. From the shape of the shadowy image reflected on the water, he knew it was Zamara.

"This is an accursed place—tunnels full of water, giant sinkholes, inhuman statues. The sooner we are out of here, the better I will like it."

"You'll get no argument from me," Kormak said.

"This would be a bad place to get caught by a sorcerer or his pet. We move too slowly and if we lose the lights, we're done."

Kormak glanced back. Some of the men held ships storm lanterns, some carried torches. It seemed like they had enough light sources but he knew how quickly things could go wrong in a place like this.

"They need light too," Kormak said.

"Do they?" Jonas asked.

"The pirates do," the captain said. "But does the sorcerer or his pet demon."

"You're a ray of blessed sunshine, captain."

Zamara laughed. "I am tired. I am wet. I am cold. And I don't mind admitting I am a trifle worried."

He meant he was scared almost witless but he could not say so in front of the men. Command must always look confident.

***

Ledges appeared on either side of the path, turning the passageway into another canal. Kormak pulled himself out of the water onto hexagonal flagstones. All around men passed their torches to others and clambered out of the murk. They set their lanterns on the edge of the ledge as they pulled themselves up. Even this brief respite from the chilly water cheered the men. Kormak guessed it was only a matter of time before cold wet clothing brought the misery back.

The waters of the tunnel rippled, as if displaced by something below the surface. A man in the channel screamed. Blood billowed out around him. The victim splashed and shrieked then disappeared below the water. When he emerged something clung to his arm. It was about the size of a man's head, teardrop shaped, with six tiny limbs and a long tail. It bore as much resemblance to the Triturids as a tadpole to a toad. It came to Kormak the things were the spawn of the city's amphibian inhabitants.

More men shrieked and stumbled in the water. Kormak reached down and grabbed one by the arm. The man howled and writhed and made it difficult for the Guardian to keep his grip. The spawn had sunk its teeth into his flesh and would not let go. Its jaws had closed like a mantrap and looked just as powerful.

"Be still!" Kormak shouted at the flailing man. He was afraid of being pulled into the water himself. Zamara's blade flashed out and skewered the little monster but it still would not let go. The screaming man twisted again and his shirt gave way. Kormak's fingers found no purchase on his slick flesh and the man disappeared below the water.

A few heartbeats later everything was still. There was no sign of the men who had vanished. Blood made the waters darker.

"We were lucky," said Frater Jonas. "They did not attack us as we crossed the main chamber. If we had all been in the water then…"

He did not need to finish that thought. It was darker now. They had lost many of the torches and lanterns.

Zamara's face looked ghastly in the dim light. Over half his command lay dead and he still had not caught sight of the man they hunted. The soldiers had a haggard desperate quality to them. They did not know what to do. They would have turned back except for the fact that no one wanted to get into the water.

"Those were the children of the things we fought above," said Jonas. "They were spawn!"

"Yes," Kormak said.

"This is a birthing chamber then. No wonder they tried so hard to keep us away. They were trying to protect the place."

"Let's hope the Kraken and his men suffered as much as we have on the way in."

"I suspect he was better prepared than we were. He had maps. He had old books. He had relics."

"He certainly spent a lot of time and effort to get here. We need to find out what for."

They fell silent. All of them were wondering what exactly could draw a man to a place like this.

CHAPTER NINE

AHEAD THE RAMP led up through a great hexagonal archway, over which a green gem, the size of a human head, glowed faintly. The arch was perhaps three times the height of a man. Two grooves marked the floor. It looked as if two halves of a doorway had receded into the wall.

Inside the chamber the floor curved downward into a bowl. A mosaic showing more images of Triturids glittered amid the stonework. Around the walls of the chamber, galleries looked down. This place might once have been an arena.

In the centre a huge idol squatted atop an altar. It looked like a Triturid: six-limbed, newt-like, with huge protruding eyes and a massive, neckless head. Its limbs were thicker and much more monstrous and each ended in huge claws. Even hunched, its head rose higher than Kormak's though he stood on the ledge.

Around its neck a balefully glowing gem hung on a copper chain. Blood splashed the statue. A dozen corpses in the motley garb of pirates sprawled around it. Something had shredded their flesh. In their midst a black-cowled figure lay. Something about the shape told Kormak it wasn't human.

"Looks like we found the Kraken's crew," said Frater Jonas.

"Some of them," said Zamara. "There's only half a dozen corpses. He should have more like fifty men."

"If they didn't die on the way in," said Jonas.

"That must be the Black Priest," Kormak said. The black-cloaked figure lay nearest to the foot of the statue. A jelly-like substance soiled its clothing.

There was no sign of anything that might have killed the pirates. If there was a trap, he had no clue as to its nature.

"You think the Quan turned on its allies?" Zamara asked. "This looks like demon work."

Jonas snorted. "How would you know what demon work looked like?"

"This was certainly not done by men, now, was it?" the captain replied.

Kormak sought clues amid the carnage. The dead men lay in the depression in the stone floor below them. They were all on the mosaic, near the monstrous idol.

"Where is the Kraken?" Zamara asked. "Where are the rest of the crew?"

Kormak studied the galleries above them. No one was visible. There were no lights. Men might be crouching down behind the balustrades. If so, what were they waiting for?

"That gem is probably what they came for?" Zamara said. He licked his lips.

"And something stopped them from getting it. Something that killed those pirates and the Quan." Jonas said.

"There's something guarding it then," said Jonas.

"In my experience there usually is in a place like this."

"It's good that you have some experience of situations like this, Sir

Kormak," said Zamara, a note of cool irony in his voice. "I'm glad someone has."

Kormak shrugged.

"And what does your vast experience suggest we should do now?" Zamara asked.

"Leave the thing well alone."

"The Kraken thought it worth coming all this way for," said Jonas.

"Just from the look of it, it's worth a king's ransom," said Zamara. Both men exchanged glances. The gem was worth a lot more than the bounty Aemon of Siderea would pay for the Kraken. They had come all this way themselves and if they could not return with the pirate's head, they could go back with something even more valuable.

"I would not do that if I were you," said Kormak. "The gem is a source of magical power. Look at the way it glows

"We do not all have your admirable capacity for self-denial, Guardian," said Zamara. "Terves go fetch the gem."

Terves looked at Kormak. Kormak shook his head. Terves looked at the priest and his captain and both of them nodded.

"A triple share for the man who brings me that gem," said Zamara.

Terves took a slow step towards the great idol. A squad of the younger soldiers, forgetting their fear, raced ahead to the idol. One of them scrambled up onto its legs and reached up to get the gem.

The statue's eyes opened. The soldiers froze.

The idol swept out a huge webbed claw and removed the head of the nearest marine. The monster reared on its two hind legs.

Zamara's mouth hung open. His eyes were wide. He swallowed and then shouted, "Fire! Fire! Fire!"

A hail of crossbow bolts hit the beast, emerging from its skin like needles from a pin-cushion. The creature opened its huge mouth, revealing endless rows of serrated teeth. A long sticky tongue flickered out and wrapped itself around another soldier, immobilising him. A second later, a huge claw swiped down, disembowelling the victim.

The huge arms descended and two more of the treasure seekers fell. Ribs crunched as the giant stood upon him, reduced flesh to jelly. The crossbowmen cranked the windlasses of their weapons, trying to draw the lines tight so they could fire again. Jonas knelt down and presented his holy symbol as he recited a prayer. Zamara shouted at his men, "Stand your ground!"

The enormous creature lumbered forwards, reached out with a huge talon and dragged another squirming soldier to its mouth. Enormous jaws snapped shut. The man's body flopped to the ground, blood spurting from the stump of his neck. The creature spat. The soldier's crushed head arced down and rolled to Kormak's feet. Eyes stared up at the Guardian in horror.

Kormak leapt into the pit. His sword swept out, catching the monster behind the ankle. The limb flopped, hamstrung. Blackish blood poured forth. Relief surged through the Guardian. The creature was a living thing at least, not an animated statue.

A massive paw swept downward. Displaced air rushed past Kormak's head as he ducked. He rolled to one side and slashed upwards with his blade. Dwarf-forged steel clove the creature's belly and sent entrails squirming forth.

The monster's four legs enabled it to remain upright despite its crippled rear limb. It twisted to face Kormak and its long tongue flickered out. Kormak's blade severed its tip. Black blood spurted into his face, hitting him in the eyes, blinding him.

By instinct he threw himself backwards as a webbed foot crashed down where he had been. He wiped at his eyes, knowing these few seconds of blindness were most likely going to cost him his life.

A war cry bellowed out from close by. The cleaver sound of a blade biting flesh filled Kormak's ears. When he had cleared his stinging eyes he saw Terves back-pedalling away from the monster, waving his blade, trying to hold its attention.

Kormak chopped two-handed at the brute's rear leg, severing it just below where the knee would have been in a man. It flopped down, massive jaw impacting the ground in front of Terves. The soldier stabbed down with his sword driving it through the creature's eye. Its head tilted to one side and it began to rear up, refusing to die.

Kormak leapt onto its slippery back and drove his blade downwards into the base of the creature's skull where the head met the spine. Vertebrae severed. The beast let out one last frantic croak, twitched and lay still. Terves stood nearby, panting. Kormak took a deep breath.

Zamara clambered down, prised open the links of the creature's collar and then pulled the gem and its setting out from below it. He gazed into its depths as if hypnotised by what he saw.

His jaw went slack and he licked his lips. "There are things inside this gem, thousands of things," he said. His face looked ghastly in the red light from the gem. He shook his head as if to clear it. "We're rich," he said. "You could buy a kingdom with this."

"And I will," said a voice from the gallery. Ironic applause rang out. Looking up Kormak saw a face peering down at him. The Kraken did indeed bear a resemblance to King Aemon. Beside him were more pirates.

The crossbowmen tried to bring their weapons to bear, but arrows streaked down at them, taking them in the stomach.

"I must thank you for your help," said the Kraken. "The Spawn

OCEAN OF FEAR | 75

Mother proved stronger than my Quan ally anticipated. Its powers worked better on the tadpoles than their parent. I confess I expected to have to re-think my plans. I had not expected such potent allies to appear. I will thank my half-brother for sending you when I claim his palace as my own."

"We have the gem. You're going to have to come down and get it," said Kormak.

"It is more than a mere gem, my friend. I would not advise you to hold onto it if you value your sanity."

"What is it?" Jonas asked.

"The Teardrop of Leviathan, lost during the ancient wars of the Elder Races. It was taken as spoils and immured here after Tritureon slew Dhagoth. It is a talisman of great magical power."

"I assume you are not going to put it to any good use," Kormak said.

"On the contrary, I am going to reclaim my birthright with it."

"First you're going to have to reclaim the gem."

"I had hoped you would see reason. You're outnumbered. You're looking a bit battered and I will spare your lives if you cooperate."

"Like you spared the lives of the people in Wood's Edge?"

"That flyspeck village? My companion needed to feed and quite honestly I would have left the damn villagers alone if they had provided me with what I requested. They declined to do so and paid the price, as you will if you don't see sense."

"I fear we must reject your kind offer," said Zamara.

"A pity." He shrugged and tossed a black egg down into the pit. The marines dived for cover. The Kraken vaulted over the barrier. His huge cloak billowed out from his shoulders, revealing the alien armour encasing his body. It was dark and chitinous, ribbed around the chest in such a way as to make it look as if the wearer's skeleton were on the outside. Black tubes emerged from the chestplate and flowed into veins of the Kraken's neck. They pulsed as if feeding on his blood.

The armour bulged and flowed in odd places as the Kraken moved. It gave the impression of being alive and grafted to its owner's body. Kormak had seen such things worn by Old Ones in the past.

The sorcerer drifted down rather than fell. A ruby ring on his left hand caught the light. Kormak had just enough time to notice this before the Kraken spoke a word of power. Clouds of inky black smoke emerged from the shattered crystal egg he had thrown. A strange peppery odour reached Kormak's nostrils and his eyes began to sting.

"Hold your breath!" Jonas shouted. "Close your eyes!"

Kormak had already started to do so. Coughs and screams sounded around him out of the darkness. His flesh crawled in anticipation of a blade stroke. He listened as he had been taught in the fighter's court on Aethelas, tried to sense any displacement of the air near him.

More shouts echoed round the chamber, in what sounded like Zamara's voice. Kormak stood ready, blade in hand, eyes stinging.

The inky blackness faded. Kormak saw men on the ground, retching and choking. Jonas stood over Zamara, his mouth covered in a handkerchief, his eyes red and watering. The Kraken was nowhere to be seen, nor was the gem nor were any of his men.

"What did he do?" Zamara asked. He was coughing and looked as if was going to be sick. "What was that mist?"

"He used an alchemical gas," said Jonas. "It obscures the vision and attacks the constitution."

The men looked ill. Most could barely stand. A few sobbed and claimed they were blind. Kormak felt dizzy and nauseous and he had only breathed in a tiny amount of the gas. His eyes felt as if he had been staring at fire for days on end. They were in no shape for a battle.

"Something ripped the gem from my hands," Zamara said.

"You were lucky. He could have killed you," Jonas said.

"It might have given away his position," said Kormak. "And I doubt his men would have done any better in the fog than we did."

Jonas nodded. "The gas would have affected them too. It's probably why he didn't order them to attack us. Why risk a fight when he did not have to?"

Zamara looked pale. "Did you see the way he fell? As if he weighed less than a feather. He should not have been able to drop from that height without breaking his legs. That was sorcery indeed."

"We have other things to worry about," said Kormak.

Most of the lights had gone out when they were dropped or spilled.

"Pick up those lanterns," Kormak shouted. "If we lose the light we'll never get out of here."

Terves lifted one of the ship's lanterns. Other soldiers gathered the remainder.

"We need to follow him!" said Zamara. "We can't let him get away."

Kormak stared pointedly at the sick soldiers. Most of them lay on the ground. A few sat with their heads between their legs. One or two of them had stopped breathing entirely. "We are in no condition to fight anybody. Most of those men can barely walk."

In truth Zamara did not look any better than his soldiers, but he cursed and ordered them to get up, get into formation. The soldiers did their best to respond. Frater Jonas moved around advising them, telling them to wash their eyes with canteen water.

Kormak went over to the cloaked form of the Black Priest. He prodded the robed form with the toe of his boot. The flesh beneath gave way in a spongy boneless fashion. He lifted the corpse by its robe and heard a gasp from Zamara and the marines. A long, greenish squid-like tentacle emerged from beneath. Suckers ran along its length. Kormak carried the body to the ramp. It felt about as heavy as an eight-year-old child. He stripped off the robes. What lay beneath was like something adapted to living on the bottom of the sea. Its flesh was cold and slimy.

It had a bulbous squid-like head. The eyes were almost human, albeit larger. A long, streamlined form stretched out from beneath the head. From where the shoulders would have been on a man two tentacles emerged. Six more emerged from the bottom of the torso. The tentacles seemed boneless, all muscle. Each of the limbs would be as strong as a constrictor snake.

The survivors of Wood's Edge had claimed the priest had seemed to drift rather than walk. Possibly it levitated like some of the Old Ones. In death, it seemed to have lost that gift. Another thought occurred to him. Perhaps the Kraken's strange armour granted a similar power. That would explain the slowness of the sorcerer's descent.

Frater Jonas came over to where he stood. "It is fascinating," he said. "I have never been so close to such a thing before. But we must go. The Kraken has a head's start on us and we need to get out of here before we lose all illumination."

Kormak nodded and the small party of soldiers limped from the chamber. They marched like men already beaten.

CHAPTER TEN

NOTHING OPPOSED THEM as they plodded through the benighted city. The spawn in the entrance tunnel appeared sated on their earlier victims. The Triturids seemingly had no interest in stopping them leaving. It looked as if they had fought only to prevent the ziggurat being invaded.

After long hours of marching they staggered up to the docks. The captain cursed. Frater Jonas made an Elder Sign over his breast. The soldiers looked grim.

The mast of the pirate vessel jutted from the water. There was no sign of the Ocean's Blade.

The bodies of the watch party floated in the river.

"Looks like the Kraken has made good his escape," said Kormak.

"He scuttled his own ship and took ours? Why?" Jonas asked.

"It was the better ship," said Zamara. "And he has made it very difficult for us to follow him."

"You're saying we're trapped here," said Jonas. His voice sounded as if it was about to crack.

"We can follow the river back to the coast and meet up with the fleet there," said Kormak.

Zamara nodded. "It's a long slow march."

"We could build rafts," said Kormak. "Going with the current would be quicker."

"We'll never catch him now."

"He still needs to get by the Marlin and the Sea Dragon," said Jonas.

"They'll see the Ocean's Blade," said Zamara. "If he's quick he'll pass them and be out into the open sea before they understand what has happened. If he has any knowledge of Siderean flag code, they might not even pursue. He can tell them to wait."

"Now we know why he took your ship," said Kormak.

"What I'd like to know is how he managed it," said Zamara. He sounded petulant. "We left enough men with the ship to hold of his crew."

"My guess would be sorcery," said Kormak.

Frater Jonas nodded agreement. "The black cloud he used against us would weaken the prize crew and give him the advantage."

Zamara nodded his head. He looked very weary. It was not easy for a Siderean captain to lose his ship. It was going to be even harder for him as a Siderean noble to return and explain what had happened to his king. To tell the truth, Kormak thought, none of them came out of this looking well.

Zamara straightened his shoulders, and began bellowing orders to the marines. The tired soldiers straightened their shoulders and prepared to march.

***

By evening, bone weary, they trudged past the boundary wall of Triturek. Elves waited in the gloom beneath the trees. All their heads swivelled at once, again giving the impression that a single intelligence glared out through multiple pairs of eyes.

"Tumitha gives you greetings," they said simultaneously.

"Greetings," Kormak said.

"Your quest did not go well," said the elves.

"The Kraken has what he sought although his Quan ally gave his life to get it."

"That much is something," said the elves.

"Much as I would like to stand and chat," said Zamara, "I have a sorcerer to pursue."

Kormak kept his expression neutral. Could the captain not see that if they antagonised the elves they would be going nowhere? Perhaps he did and just did not care.

"You lose no time by being civil to us," said the elves. "We can provide you with rivercraft since you require them. We can provide you with extra arms to row them. Your enemy is our enemy."

"Perhaps you should have remembered that when we entered the city," said Zamara. "With your help we might have been able to stop the sorcerer."

"It is a place we do not go. We do not wish to be tainted by it."

"Yet you let us go in."

"That was your choice," said the elves. Their multiple voices were bland. "To stop you we would have had to fight you and that would have gained us nothing save the laughter of our enemy."

"We accept your offer gratefully," said Kormak. Before Zamara could say anything more, he looked at the captain and said, "With your aid we may yet be able to overtake our foe and regain our ship."

Zamara remained quiet, for which Kormak was thankful.

***

The elvish canoes were large. Their crews worked with an eerie precision, their movements far more synchronised than any human oarsmen. They had left space in the centre of the craft for the marines and would not accept any aid with the rowing. They guided their craft swiftly with the current, moving effortlessly.

Ralan sat beside Kormak on the prow of one vessel. "So you killed the Triturid Mother in her spawning pool," he said. "You have ended an ancient race unless a new Mother emerges. It seems you have achieved the Quan's vengeance for them."

Kormak's expression was grim. "That was not the only work I did for them. I let the Kraken get what he came for."

The elf's green eyes turned on him. "What was that?"

Kormak described the gem. The elf's brow crinkled into a frown. The depthless wisdom of Tumitha glittered in his eyes. "That is an ill thing."

"What is it?"

"Your words paint a picture of an Eldrim aether matrix."

"That means nothing to me."

"Such crystals are a concentration of pure aether, distilled and solidified magical energy. They are sources of enormous power. They were often used as focuses for the most potent spell engines."

"It goes without saying such an object could be useful to a sorcerer," said Jonas.

The elves nodded. "If he knows how to tap it, it would give him the sort of power that has not been seen in a long age of this world. But only the Old Ones knew how to do that."

Kormak said, "Human sorcerers study the works of the Old Ones. The Kraken sought this thing out over a number of years. I think it's fair to assume he knows something about using it or why else would he seek it?"

"Then he will be a menace to all who live."

"Unless he is stopped," said Kormak.

The elves all nodded. "Indeed. Unless he is stopped," they said in unison. Their gaze lingered on Kormak as if weighing whether he was the man to do it.

***

They smelled the sea before they saw it. There was a tang of salt in the air that warred with the scent of the forest. Gulls shrieked overhead, white dots on a blue sky.

"It would be best if we left you before the river's mouth," said Ralan. "I would not wish to risk a misunderstanding with the crews of your warships out yonder in that great blue desert."

"We thank you for your aid," Kormak said.

The elf looked at him. For once there was no suggestion of the vast presence of Tumitha behind his eyes. "It is nothing. The Great Tree wishes it were more. It troubles her to think of a mortal sorcerer walking abroad with the power of the Teardrop of Leviathan to call upon."

"We have at least made good time," Kormak said. The elves had paddled through day and night, tireless and able to navigate through the darkness when humans would have made camp. Enforced inactivity had given the soldiers time to sleep and to recover from the ill-effects of the Kraken's sorcerous mist.

"The ship of your enemies is but a few hours ahead of you."

Kormak did not need to ask how the elf knew this. Tumitha was linked to countless beasts and birds in her realm. She could borrow all of their eyes and so could the elves who served her. "We shall leave you the canoes so that you can find your way to your vessels."

They angled towards the riverbank. No words had passed

between the elves. Everything was done in the same uncanny silence. The marines looked at each other, wondering what was going on.

"We're almost at the sea," Kormak shouted. "They are leaving us to go on alone."

Despite the aid the elves had given them there was an almost palpable sense of relief. The humans had been uncertain of the elves, of their inhuman endurance, of their ability to communicate with each other without speaking. They had not known whether they were allies or prisoners.

The elves pulled the canoes up to the riverbank and without a word of farewell, disappeared into the forest.

"That was odd," said Zamara. "They are not the politest of people are they?"

"They gave us aid when we needed it," said Kormak. "That is all the politeness I require."

Zamara nodded and contemplated the much-diminished number of soldiers under his command. Some of them lay in the canoes still, feverish from their wounds, or the effects of the gas. He wondered if they would ever recover fully.

"I am thankful to them," said Frater Jonas. "But I will be even more grateful to get back aboard our ships and be gone from this place."

Zamara looked at Kormak. "The Ocean's Blade cannot have made much better time than we did. We might still catch it if we are quick." He looked a lot more hopeful. The opportunity to erase his failure had been given to him and he seemed determined to seize it.

He marched around the soldiers, kicking them to their feet, shouting orders, telling them that soon they would have ship's biscuit and rum. That thought got the marines back into the canoes and pulling at the oars.

Kormak sat at the back of one of the small boats. The river widened. The ocean became visible. Ahead he could see the masts of two warships. There was no sign of a third.

***

They rowed closer under the suspicious eyes of the crew of the Marlin. The ballista was aimed at them as were scores of crossbows. The sight of the long low elvish canoes with the green eyes painted on their prow caused disquiet.

Zamara stood on the prow with his hands upraised, giving everyone a chance to see him. Captain Dominic, the master of the Marlin shouted a halloo. A few minutes later they were scrambling up the netting on the ships side.

Zamara greeted Captain Dominic. "Have you seen the Ocean's Blade?"

"No," said the Marlin's master, unease in his tone.

"She cannot have been too far ahead of us."

"A strange mist rose over the river mouth this morning. The lookouts claimed they heard something but we could not see anything."

Zamara cursed. Frater Jonas said, "Sorcery. The work of the Shadow."

"You saw nothing?" said Kormak.

Dominic shook his head. "Until we saw you."

"They could have gone anywhere," said Jonas.

"No," Kormak said. "The Kraken has found what he was looking for."

"He may be returning home to Port Blood, to plot his next move," said Frater Jonas.

"We don't know that," said Zamara. "He could just as easily be heading south to plunder the coasts of Siderea."

"We don't know anything. We're guessing," said Kormak.

"He has something within his power that would make him a prince among sorcerers once he masters it," said Jonas. "It will take him some time to do so. He will want to be in a place of safety while he tries."

"That is your considered opinion, is it?" Zamara asked.

"It is."

"Very well then, we shall head west towards the Pirate Islands." He seemed glad to be able to push the responsibility off onto somebody else. If they failed, there would be someone else to share in the blame. The way politics and personal ambition had intruded here disgusted Kormak.

"Get a man aloft," said Zamara to Captain Dominic. "I want someone scanning the horizon every minute of every hour until we catch sight of the Ocean's Blade or until we make landfall."

"Aye, aye, sir," said Captain Dominic. The expression on his face told Kormak that Dominic was uneasy. He had reason to be. The Pirate Isles were not a place where the King of Siderea's sailors were likely to be welcomed.

***

The land receded behind them. Sailing on the Marlin was a very different experience from being on the canoe or the Ocean's Blade. The great cog relied on her sails for propulsion. Such was her size that the sweeps in her side were useful only for warping her into harbour. Zamara had assured him that on the high seas, when the wind was with them, it should be at least as fast as the war-galley.

The Marlin stood much higher in the water than a galley. The view over the figurehead on the prow allowed Kormak to see much further. Not that there was much to view. Ahead of them lay endless leagues of ocean. Only the ripple of the waves and the sight of the gulls broke the monotony. He began to understand the fear many sailors had, that once out of sight of land they would be lost. There were no landmarks, nothing except the horizon and the clouds.

"Not so," said Jonas when he expressed his misgivings. "The captain can navigate by the position of the sun and by the stars. He keeps logs of his journeys and descriptions of the currents. He has a magnetic stone to set our bearings by. We will be able to return, the Holy Sun willing."

Kormak understood the basic principles of navigation but that seemed optimistic. Jonas smiled, "As long as the captain can find east we can always go back the way we came and eventually we will find land. It would be hard to miss an entire continent and that is what lies to our rear."

"And what lies ahead?" Kormak asked.

"The whole vast ocean," said the priest. "The Sunken Kingdoms, the lost lands of the Solari, archipelagos of thousands of islands, stretching all the way to the Seven Duchies in Terra Nova. Men have sailed these seas before. Men have crossed this ocean before. There is nothing to be afraid of."

"Then why do you sound as if you are speaking as much to reassure yourself as to reassure me?"

Jonas laughed. "Perhaps because I am. We have not set ourselves an easy task. If we do not overhaul the Kraken before he reaches the waters of the Pirate Islands then our mission will fail. Two warships will not be enough to let us storm into the harbour and take the Kraken."

"I know," said Kormak. "I have been there before."

"You are a well-travelled man," said Jonas.

"I go where the Holy Sun sends me."

"Why did he send you to Port Blood?"

"To hunt down a servant of the Old Ones who had fled there."

"You succeeded, of course. Or you would not be here now."

"I killed it," he said. He did not like the memories that flooded back into his mind. "Port Blood is not a pleasant place."

"I doubt a city full of pirates could be."

Kormak's eyes narrowed. "Pirates are like other men. I've seen unpaid soldiers plunder. It takes less than you think to make an armed man become a bandit."

"Is that the voice of experience talking?"

Kormak looked sidelong at the priest. The menace in his glance made Frater Jonas look away.

"If, by experience, you mean that I have met such men, the answer is yes. If you mean have I been one, the answer is no."

"I never meant to suggest you had performed any criminal act," said Jonas. "But we were talking of Port Blood. How did you get there?"

"Certain merchant ships sailing out of Solarea and Siderea go there."

"This I know. Even the King-Emperor of Siderea deals with the pirates when it suits him."

"I took a ship there and I remained behind when it left. Port Blood is a lawless enough place. They do not keep track of strangers. Most end up with their throats cut. A man with no crew or no friends has a short life in the pirate city unless he is good with a blade."

"And you are very good with a blade. You are thinking that you might have to visit Port Blood again, if we do not overhaul the Kraken, are you not?"

"If need be, I can be dropped off in a small boat and make landfall on the island. There are places where you can do that, if you know what you are about."

"If worst comes to worst, I may join you."

"I do not think I can guarantee your safety," said Kormak.

"I can look after myself, if I must," said the priest.

"Why are you so desperate to catch the Kraken?" Kormak asked.

"I am loyal to King Aemon and his brother. And I fear what this madman is up to."

"That would seem wise."

Jonas paused for a moment then said, "I have been studying those books we found in the Kraken's cabin."

"I wondered what you were doing in your berth all day."

"They are mostly spell books but there were some entries that were more in the nature of a journal. The Kraken was very keen to get his hands on the Teardrop."

"I think we both know why."

"Do we? I am not so sure. There are other entries in some form of code."

"It is a pity we cannot read his notes then." Kormak let the words hang in the air. He had his suspicions about Frater Jonas.

The priest gave him a slow smile. "I have some skill in cyphering. My Order uses its own codes and in the past I have broken others. Given time I may be able to work out the contents of his journals."

"That might be useful."

The distant sky was darkening.

"It will be night soon," said Frater Jonas. "We may be able to see the running lights of the Ocean's Blade."

"If she is showing any."

"We are a long way out over the sea. Why would the Kraken suspect pursuit now? As far as he knows we are still stuck at Triturek."

"He is a cautious man. I think we have already established that," said Kormak.

"And mayhap he has supernatural sources of information." Frater Jonas turned away. "I will return to the books," he said. "If I find out anything I will let you know."

"Be sure you do," said Kormak. He watched the smaller man shuffle away, shoulders bowed and wondered whether Jonas would pass on any information he found.

CHAPTER ELEVEN

"SAIL HO!" THE cry rang out from the crow's nest of the Marlin. Zamara raced towards the mainmast and swarmed up it. Once he reached the lookout post, he produced his telescope and looked off into the distance. His figure became rigid with tension, a hunting dog scenting prey. After five days at sea, he had all but given up hope but now...

Moments later he slid down the rope. As he swept past Kormak to the command deck, he said, "It's the Ocean's Blade. I would know her lines anywhere. If the wind stays with us, we will overhaul her before the day is out. Best ready your blade, Master Guardian. We will have need of it."

Slowly, the sail of the Ocean Blade rose above the horizon. From the Marlin's prow, Kormak made out the distant outline of the ship on the horizon. The waves were bigger now. The sea and sky were greyer. The wind was stronger. The oars could not drive the pirate craft through the swells as efficiently as the cog's great sails. Its smaller spread of canvas could not make up the difference.

Frater Jonas joined Kormak on the foredeck. They had become quite companionable over the past few days; the only men aboard who did not have crew duties. Jonas claimed to have made some progress on the Kraken's cypher but not to have broken it. He gave a very good impression of a man frustrated by his own slow progress. Contemplating the enemy ship, he looked thoughtful.

The priest said, "As soon as he realises he cannot outrun us, he will turn at bay. The Ocean's Blade's ram could easily hole and sink us."

"I don't think our captain is going to allow that."

Zamara shouted orders to the engineers. They winched the catapults at stern and forecastles to tautness and stacked firepots near them. The same thing was occurring on the Sea Dragon. In order to close with her pursuers, the Ocean's Blade would have to run the gauntlet of intense missile fire. It would be a race to see whether she could be sunk before she made contact.

"If he gets that close we can board," said Kormak. "Even if he sinks the Marlin we can take back the Ocean's Blade or swim to the Sea Dragon."

"Those of us who can swim," said Jonas. "Many sailors cannot. They believe that it merely prolongs the agony of a man before he drowns. They think that if Saa-Aquor, the Mistress of the Deeps, wants a man she will claim him."

The Ocean's Blade showed no sign of turning at bay. As the long day wore on the reason became clear. A low smudge on the horizon indicated the presence of land. Birds appeared in the sky. Bits of flotsam drifted in the sea nearby.

"The Pirate Islands," said Jonas. "If we go much closer we will be sighted and corsair ships will come to meet us, then we will be the ones hunted."

Kormak shaded his eyes with his hand. "I am more concerned with what the Kraken is up to on the sterncastle of his ship. Lend me your spyglass, please."

He stretched out the telescope's cylinders, rotating them until the rear of the Ocean's Blade leapt into view. The Kraken stood alone on the command deck.

The man's regal bearing was as unmistakable, as was the strange living armour wrapped around his torso. There had been one change. The Teardrop of Leviathan now blazed on the centre of his chest, as if set in the living armour.

The Kraken spread his arms wide and threw his head back. He seemed to be chanting.

Kormak's hand went to the amulet beneath his armour. They were too far from the trireme for it to have grown warm with the eddy currents of magic but he did not doubt that, had they been closer, it would even now be becoming hot.

"What is it?" Frater Jonas asked.

"He's working sorcery," Kormak said.

The waves to the rear of the Ocean's Blade seethed. A monstrous shape rose from the depths. Shouts from the sailors all around Kormak told him that they had noticed it too.

A huge head emerged, streams of water cascading down its side, running off gigantic slitted eyes that gazed up with a near worshipful air at the Kraken.

Greenish-black tentacles stretched skyward. They looked able to pull a ship the size of the Ocean's Blade below the water without difficulty.

"Our sorcerer has called his namesake," said Jonas. His tone attempted the ironic but fear lurked beneath.

"I wonder what he intends to do with it," Kormak said.

"Come, Sir Kormak, you know just as well as I do what that

maniac plans."

As if to give emphasis to his words, the giant head disappeared below the water. The tentacles sank out of sight heartbeats later. A white line appeared beneath the waves and a trail of bubbles moved in the direction of the Marlin. Ahead of it, a massive wave rose as if something huge was displacing the water.

Sailors shrieked. At this speed, it would not take long for the great creature to cover the distance between the two ships.

Zamara shouted orders. The catapults rotated on their great circular platforms. Flasks of incendiary chemicals dropped into place. The enormous arms of the war-engines whipped forward, sending their missiles spinning out over the ocean to drop in the path of the onrushing giant squid.

The shots missed. The chief engineer shouted instructions, adjusting range and tension. Another shot arced out. This time it hit the onrushing mass but nothing happened. A yellow glow showed under the water but the monster kept coming closer.

"Alchemical fire," said Frater Jonas. "I am not sure that even that will work."

The glow vanished and the white wake faded out. A few of the crew raised a panicked cheer, relief evident in their voices.

"Or perhaps I was wrong," said Jonas. He wiped his brow. They studied the empty sea for long minutes.

The ship shivered, as if it had encountered an obstruction beneath its waterline. A scraping sound rose from below.

Colour drained from the priest's face. The ship vibrated again. Had it risen by more than the natural ebb and flow of the waves?

The Marlin shook as if in the grip of a storm. The scraping sounded much louder now. Out of the water, serpent-like, rose a tentacle as large as a ghost snake. Leech mouths covered it. They dilated and shut again with an odd sucking sound.

The hull gave a tortured shriek. Timbers splintered as the sea around the Marlin became alive with gigantic tentacles. They descended on the ship with irresistible force, smashing through the carved wooden handrails, tore lanyards, pulled down sails. Some of the tentacles were shrivelled like slugs exposed too long to the sun. Yellowish fluid dripped from them, traces of the alchemical fire sticking to the flesh that not even the waters of the deep could remove.

Kormak dived to one side. A suckered limb thicker than his torso smashed into the deck beside him. His sword erupted from its scabbard. Dwarf-forged steel slashed the tentacle, carving through thick skin to reveal the slick white meat beneath.

More and more missiles arced from the Sea Dragon. Men fired their crossbows at the tentacles. The waters around the Marlin were slick and black. The stink of burning wood arose as the alchemical fires transferred from the flesh of the monster to the planking of the ship.

The deck shivered, as if the Marlin had been hit by an enormous hammer. From beneath came the sound of timbers smashing. A spurt of water bubbled up through the planks. Part of the deck gave way as another massive tentacle smashed through it. Looking into the gap yawning at his feet, Kormak could see the enormous eyes and hungry maw of the great squid. Agonised madness glittered in its gaze. It focused on him and the tentacle came smashing down.

Kormak leapt to one side as the deck splintered. Water filled the hold of the ship where the beast had broken through. The Marlin was doomed. All that was left for its crew was to dive into the water and hope to evade the creature's thrashing limbs.

Wild rage flickered through Kormak's mind. He sprang down

into the hold. His booted legs smashed into the squid's giant rubbery head. His razor sharp blade drove down through its eye and into its brain. A weird hissing shriek emerged from the squid's beak. Its limbs thrashed. Kormak turned his sword in the jelly of the eye then pulled it free with a sucking sound. He sprang upwards to grab the torn edge of the deck with his free hand and hauled himself over.

Tentacles smashed against the Marlin like the flailing limbs of a dozen maddened drummers. Wood splintered, the hull shattered and the hungry sea poured in. Men jumped into the water, frantically trying to pull clear of the ship before the suction of its sinking dragged them under. Kormak sheathed his blade and dived. He was most likely doomed. The weight of his armour and blade would drown him just as easily as the undertow from the great cog going down.

There was no easy way to get the armour off and his every instinct protested letting go off his sword. He kicked out, trying to keep himself up in the water. He saw the small boat that had been attached to the rear of the Marlin, pulling closer. A soaking wet Frater Jonas was in it. He reached out with an oar. Kormak grabbed it and with the priest's help scrambled aboard.

"That was well-timed," Kormak said. At any moment, he half-expected a mass of tentacles to break the surface of the water and begin pulling victims down into the depths.

The enormous form of the Sea Dragon loomed over them. Men pulled themselves up the netting on its sides and into the ship.

Sailors dropped knotted ropes into the water.

Kormak dragged himself up. Frater Jonas did the same. The waterproof satchel containing the Kraken's secrets was slung over his back. The priest seemed determined to hold onto them at all costs.

***

Zamara looked ever more haggard as he strode the quarterdeck. He had stripped off his soaking wet clothing and wore only britches and his Elder Sign. His dismay was understandable. He was going to have to go back and face his king and explain how he had lost two very expensive warships in pursuit of a pirate. If Zamara did not come back with the Kraken's head he might as well not come back at all.

Frater Jonas looked gloomy.

"It was a demon of the deep," Terves said. "It rose and damn near dragged us all down into a watery hell."

Zamara rounded on him, as if he wanted to curse the man, but his self-control reasserted itself. He extended a hand to the captain of the Sea Dragon and took his spyglass, focusing it on the distant outline of the Ocean's Blade. The trireme had taken advantage of the struggle to open the distance between it and its pursuers. Kormak was surprised. He had half-expected the Kraken to come back and try and finish them off.

Zamara let out a long seaman's oath then ordered the crew to search for more survivors. He was not leaving any man of his to be marooned out here. It was a gesture calculated to endear him to his crew. It seemed he had already worked out that they could not overhaul the Ocean's Blade before it reached Port Blood.

A sense of despondency settled on the ship. The whole crew knew that the long chase was over and that there would not be any prize money for them. Zamara slumped against the sternpost, deep in thought. Father Jonas called for his attention and he and Kormak were given permission to come onto the command deck.

"We have lost the Kraken," said the captain. "And I have lost my flagship and the lives of a lot of good men."

"We can still take the Kraken," said Frater Jonas.

Zamara raised an eyebrow. "How? By sailing into the harbour of Port Blood? Three score and ten pirate vessels will give us a warmer welcome than we gave that squid. Not to mention the two great harbour forts. No, the only way we'll get the Kraken is if we come back with the King's fleet and the assembled fleets of a couple of allied nations."

"I was not thinking about a head-on assault," said Jonas.

"That's good, for I would have thought you mad if you were. What exactly, pray, do you have in mind?"

"Sir Kormak and I will go ashore and take the pirate's head."

"By this I take it you mean Sir Kormak will do the beheading while you watch and applaud. Or do you mean to challenge the pirate-sorcerer to single combat yourself?"

"I will be in an advisory capacity."

Zamara looked at him and laughed. After a while it dawned on him that the priest was serious. "You are not without courage," Zamara said. "I'll give you that, but your life won't be worth a drunkard's cuss if you're caught."

"It's a risk we're going to have to take."

Zamara looked at Kormak and said, "I can understand why he is going. The mark of the killer is written all over him, and unless I miss my guess, this won't be the first time he's murdered a man by stealth. But why do you need to go?"

"Because I have knowledge that might prove useful and I have contacts in Port Blood. And because I started this thing and I want to see it finished.

"How do you plan to get into Port Blood?"

"Simple enough," said Kormak. "Under cover of night you can take us in as close as you can, and the ship's boat can bear us to shore."

"You don't have a problem with the priest tagging along with you?"

Kormak wondered exactly why the man wanted to go into Port Blood when he could stay aboard the Sea Dragon in relative safety. "Not if he does not get in my way."

"On your own head be it then," said Zamara. "I don't think I'll be able to wait too long out here for you."

"I've found my way back from Port Blood before, captain. I imagine I will be able to do it again."

He wished he was as confident as he sounded.

CHAPTER TWELVE

THE MOON'S LIGHT turned the ocean's waves silver and black. They broke softly against the side of the small boat, rocking it in the water. In the distance, the Pirate Island was a black smear on the horizon. Kormak checked his gear. This time he had left his armour wrapped in waterproof leather. His sword was on his back. If need be, he could swim to the shore. Frater Jonas had taken off his priestly robes and wore only a simple sailor's garb. He had a package concealed within his tunic. As he had suspected, the Kraken's notes had not gone down with the Marlin. Those papers went everywhere Jonas did.

Above them Zamara stood on the deck of the Sea Dragon. "Good luck, gentlemen," he said. He could not resist place an ironic flourish on the word *gentlemen.*

"And to you, captain," said Kormak, bending to the oars of the small craft. He pulled the boat towards the distant shoreline, while the silent black shape of the cog disappeared in the gloom astern.

Frater Jonas gazed backwards for a long time. There was a thoughtful air about him at this moment. "We're a long way from Siderea," he said.

"We're a long way from anywhere."

"You think we'll ever get home?"

"Define home."

"For you it must surely be Mount Aethelas."

"I have not seen the Mountain in years. I don't expect to see it for years more."

"You've spent your whole life wandering then?"

"Most of it. It's what's expected of a Guardian. You go where your oaths take you."

The priest made a soft tut-tutting sound in the darkness. His white teeth were visible in the gloom. "You must have led an interesting life."

"If you don't mind, I would rather save my breath for rowing, unless you would prefer to scull and I will chat."

"You are better built for this duty. I saw what you did when the squid attacked today by the way. It was an act of astonishing bravery. Do you always run towards monsters with your sword in your hand?"

"Only when I want to kill them."

Jonas laughed then after a moment became serious again. "I wonder what the Kraken is up to right now."

"If I could tell you that I would be a better sorcerer than he."

"It troubles me what he intends with the Teardrop of Leviathan. He has gone to enormous lengths to acquire it. In my experience sorcerers rarely do that without very good reasons."

"Or very bad ones."

"He summoned his namesake from the depth to destroy us. It might have worked too, had not the engineers got lucky with that flask of alchemical fire and had not you decided to stab the thing through its eye."

"I think that was certainly his intention. I think we were lucky to escape."

"Let us hope our luck continues."

"Indeed." The shore was closer now. Kormak could see the white crests of the waves where they washed up against the beach, hear their quiet breaking. He waited until he felt the oar hit bottom then jumped out into water as high as his knee. Within a few seconds he had the boat on the shore. Jonas got out and they pulled it up and away from the beach to hide it in amongst the sand.

"What now?" Jonas asked.

"We walk west along the beach until we come to Port Blood. It won't take us long to find it or for it to find us."

***

It took them no more than an hour of walking to reach the hills above Port Blood harbour. The sky was clear. The weather was warm and had it not been for the knowledge of where they were headed Kormak would have found it a pleasant stroll.

They crossed the brow of a hill. Below them lay the city. From the heights it looked like a string of brilliant gems strewn around a vast dark mirror. The blazing lights of the buildings and the reflected hulls of the pirate vessels were visible in the water. Every hill and every valley seemed crammed with illuminations. In the water between the two headlands framing the harbour were multiple islands and all of them blazed in the night.

"Those are the palaces of the Fleet Captains," Kormak said. "They are the richest and most powerful of the corsairs. There's ten of them and they are all deadly, for only the very strongest can hold onto those islands. We'll head in down by the East Gate and see if we can find a drinking den for the rest of the night."

Jonas said, "We'd best be careful that we don't lose the Kraken. He might set sail again."

"He might but his crew won't like it. They're back in port and they may well have money. If they don't they can borrow it. Every man-jack of them down there will be spending like there's no tomorrow."

"For some of them there won't be."

"Which is why they are living it up while they can. A man can't spend his gold when he is hanging from the end of a rope."

"A suitable philosophy for a pirate," said Jonas.

"And for more men than pirates."

"I defer to your wisdom on such matters, Sir Kormak."

"Let's get down into the city before the sun comes up. If they see us here, they might ask what two such strangers are doing coming from inland. Most everybody reaches Port Blood by sea."

They marched down the hill.

***

There was no real East Gate because there was no wall. Fortified buildings stood with their backs to the hill line. Arrow-slit windows looked outward and away from the pirate city. There were a few entrances, long streets that ran all the way down to the harbour and the ships.

From up ahead came the sounds of raucous drunken laughter. Men with swords strapped to their hips staggered into the streets. Some supported each other as they reeled back to ship or lodging. Some brawled with fists or knives while crowds looked on and placed bets. No one paid the slightest attention to Kormak or Jonas.

The Guardian wore his sword on his waist. With just his light leather tunic on he could have been a marine from any pirate ship. The priest looked like a somewhat nervous seaman.

Blue, green and red lanterns burned in a hundred tavern

windows. Women in low-cut dresses beckoned to them as they passed. Tough looking men eyed them as if contemplating robbery.

"It's like Trefal on a feastday night when the Treasure Fleet is in," said Jonas.

"Just another merry evening in Port Blood," said Kormak. "They've got gold and they don't know whether they will be alive in a week or a moon so they spend it."

"And there's plenty here to help them do it," said Jonas.

"It's not much different from any other port I've been to. We'd best find a place to hole up for the night and you can try and get in touch with your contact in the morning."

"Pick a door," said Jonas. "I doubt any of these places are much different from the other."

Kormak strode into a smaller tavern and looked around. Men diced and played knucklebones in a corner. A good-looking red-haired woman garbed only in a diaphanous silk skirt and strategically placed scarves danced on the table while musicians played pipes and drums. Drunken sailors stomped their feet and clapped and cheered. Kormak strode up to the bar.

"You got rooms?"

The villainous looking landlord stared at him. "You got silver?"

"Yes."

"Then we got rooms."

"Let's take a look."

"Picky sort, are you?" There was a note of menace in his voice.

"What if I am?" Meaningful looks passed between the landlord, the barman and the two burly men at either end of the bar. Kormak tapped the hilt of his sword with the tips of his fingers. He wanted them to know he was sober and could use a blade.

The landlord said, "Silver gets you a berth in the common room."

Kormak shrugged. He did not mind. There was more chance of petty theft but less chance of getting your throat slit while you slept in the common rooms of a place like this. "Fine by me."

They moved down a short low corridor. Kormak kept close to the landlord and moved warily. He had known inns where a man was asking for a bludgeon to the head if he stepped through such doors. If anyone tried it here, they would find him more than ready.

The common room was long with a low ceiling and a score of hammocks hung from hooks in the walls. A couple copulated beneath a blanket in the far corner.

"You seen enough?"

Jonas looked at their surroundings appalled. Kormak nodded.

"Payment's in advance. I can stow your gear for you for a copper."

Kormak shook his head. "I carry all I own, all the time."

"Man can get his throat cut that way in Port Blood."

"Anyone who feels like making the effort is welcome to try."

"You're a hard man, eh?"

"Hard enough."

"What ship you on?"

"That's my business."

The landlord stared at him. There seemed to be something about Kormak that puzzled him. "You've the manners of a captain and yet you're staying in a seaman's lodgings," he said.

"I have my reasons."

"As you say." The landlord left.

"I think he suspects us," said Jonas.

"What can he suspect us of? We're on an island. Nobody gets here save those the corsairs allow or the corsairs themselves."

"I am worried about having my throat cut this night."

"This is an easy town for that to happen in," said Kormak. He threw himself into a hammock and fell asleep with his hand on his scabbard.

***

His sleep was restless. Men and women came and went all night, and every one of them brought him to wakefulness. A passing stranger pretended to stumble and made a fumbling exploration of his backpack until he felt Kormak's knife at his throat. He departed from the room in haste.

In the morning, Jonas looked tired. He yawned and said, "I did not get much sleep."

"Complaining about it won't help. Let's get something to eat and be about our business."

They ate scrambled eggs and bacon at a table on the veranda of the inn. It gave them a view of long low buildings built from a mix of wood and stone. Covered verandas ran the length of the muddy streets.

There were few riders and fewer carts. Most freight seemed to be carried by manacled humans, slaves taken by the pirates. The wealthier citizens rode around in litters. Drunks lay in the mud, some with a stillness that suggested that they would never rise again. Bunches of armed men swaggered along. Each group wore a different colour or had a scarf containing a different symbol draped somewhere on head, throat or arm. They were the identifying marks of different crews loyal to a captain, an admiral or a fleet.

There were men and women from every corner of the Sunlands and beyond, and more than just men. Kormak saw one or two of the Lost, elves who had broken their connection with their home forest.

There were giants and even a few orcs, which was unusual, for most of their kind hated and feared the sea. He watched them all with eager curiosity.

"It's good to have something other than ship's biscuit," said Jonas. "Although at these prices our host should have laid on a feast."

Kormak glanced around at the few diners who shared the veranda. They all had the look of men wanting fried food to go with their hangover. "It's what the customers want and what they can afford," he said.

"You seem happy enough," said Jonas.

"Like you, I am pleased to be eating something other than ship's biscuit."

"It's a lot quieter through the day, isn't it?"

"Everybody's inside sleeping off last night. By noon, they'll be ready to start again."

"Well, we have business to attend to," said Jonas. "Pleasant as this feast has been. I've got to go pay a visit to my contacts here." It was obvious from the priest's manner that he did not want the Guardian accompanying him.

"We meet back here this evening then," said Kormak.

"As you say."

CHAPTER THIRTEEN

KORMAK STROLLED THROUGH the streets. As the sun rose higher in the sky the city woke. More and more men staggered from taverns, rooming houses and mansions and made their way to the docks. More and more slaves carried bigger and bigger loads along the streets. Armed men strode everywhere, eyeing each other like dogs from rival packs, hailing comrades and friends, diving into taverns and coffee houses.

Kormak heard a surprising number of deals being made as he walked. Despite the city's reputation, merchants from all across the Kingdoms of the Sun and from far beyond came here to trade. They could pick up cargoes for a fraction of their normal price.

Kormak enjoyed the sights of the city; the long low buildings, the sprawling taverns, the large, ostentatious mansions of the rich. He liked the air of freedom about the place. Something about it appealed to a part of him he tried to suppress. He reminded himself of the ruins of Wood's Edge. That was what this sort of freedom led to.

He followed the meandering streets all the way down to the harbour, noticing more and more because he chose to, all the unattractive aspects of the city—the piles of refuse in the streets, the sprawled sots, the unburned corpses, the frightened faces of the slaves, and the nervousness of the merchants.

A tall, stern faced man strode by him with a dozen cutthroats in tow. His manner showed he was a captain, as self-important as any Siderean nobleman, and in his own way, quite as powerful. Captains owned ships and their crews formed bands of warriors as fierce as any knight's retainers and just as devoted for as long as their captain remained successful. The man noticed Kormak looking at him and stared back, a challenge in his stare.

With an effort of will, Kormak kept walking, ignoring the sudden burst of laughter behind him. He was not here to fight with some jumped-up cockerel. He had a mission and he needed to be about it.

***

Port Blood harbour was huge, a sheltered bay enfolded by two promontory arms. A tower stood at each point of the so-called Claws. In fogs they became lighthouses, in sieges, strongpoints.

Small islands dotted the bay. Each contained a mansion as big as a palace and as defensible as a keep. A forest of masts rose above the multiple piers. Small boats moved everywhere. Great warehouses lined the sea front.

A giant slave, half again Kormak's height, with shoulders as broad as Kormak's outstretched arms, strode by carrying a pole the size of a small tree-trunk. Cages of parrots hung from either end. The birds peered at him with bright mad eyes. The giant had the slow, somnolent look that gelding always gave their race. He bore no resemblance to the ferocious warriors from the cold lands Kormak had fought in his youth.

Taverns dotted the waterfront. Some of them rose above the water itself, timber structures, built on stilt-like pylons, joined to the land by carved wooden bridges, with verandas on their edges from which a man could study the harbour. Kormak picked one and strode inside.

He ordered a beer and looked out to sea. Ships came and went, under sail and under oar. The air of a bustling port hovered over the city. Tidal waves of wealth flowed through Port Blood and men made money every step of the way.

"Sure and it's a grand sight, isn't it?" said the bartender.

"That it is," said Kormak.

"You looking for a place on a ship?"

"I might be?"

"You have the look of a fighting man."

"I should hope so. I have spent my whole life at it."

"Fall out with your previous captain, did you? Not that it's any of my business."

"Something like that. Who is hiring?"

"There's Blane of the Sea Swallow, good ship. He's looking for men. There's Timon of the Axe Raider—they say he's lucky and to tell the truth I think they are right. There's Marselus of the Storm Petrel. He's always looking for men who can use a blade."

"They all drink here, do they?"

The barman smiled. "Sometimes, when they come in off a voyage, and they stand their crew a grog or two."

"And the bartender as well, no doubt."

"Aye."

"Have one yourself then."

"Don't mind if I do, sir. I am certain the owner won't mind since I am he." He poured a small tot of grog into a jug and clinked glasses with Kormak.

"How about the Kraken?" The Guardian asked.

The temperature in the room cooled. "Not that I would speak ill of any captain but why would you want to be going on a sorcerer's ship?"

"I'm not saying I want to sail with him. I am just curious."

"A bad thing to be curious about, sir, and no mistake. Those that are curious about the Kraken tend to be found floating in the harbour. He keeps himself to himself, never speaks at the Council of Captains. Never comes into a city tavern and stands a round, and his crew are a grim lot."

"They say he's just returned to the city."

"They say right—he came in yesterday, riding a new ship, a sweet looking trireme, Siderean I would judge by the lines."

"That's what I had heard."

"The oddest thing was that he sailed off in another galley, not the Kraken's Reach. That's his flagship and a monstrous size of one too."

"Maybe he went somewhere where he needed a vessel that did not draw much water. Upriver somewhere maybe."

"Such was the speculation," said the bartender. "He's a deep one the Kraken is and he keeps his schemes to himself."

"In any case he found a new ship or took it in battle. His crew is hard enough and he works all kinds of magic or so they say."

"I've heard that he can call his namesake from the bottom of the sea."

The bartender shrugged, uncomfortable with this topic of conversation. "That would not surprise me. It's not the only thing he calls from the dark waters. He keeps company with the Dwellers in the Deep."

"Who would they be?"

"Old Ones, sir, or so they say. They inhabited the seas around here afore ever the Old Kingdoms sank. Some of their descendants dwell in the lost cities yet."

Kormak looked at him. He made his expression disbelieving.

"I'm just telling you what Rhiana and the other divers tell me. They're the ones who make a living plundering the drowned ruins."

"And how would they do that?"

"They're the deep divers, sir, not me. You would have to ask them."

"Where would I find this Rhiana?"

The bartender was suspicious now. He was wondering what Kormak was really after. "Along the waterfront or on the Blue Boy if it's in harbour."

"Thanks," Kormak said.

The bartender pursed his lips. He seemed to have come to a conclusion about Kormak. "They never share their real secrets with the likes of you and me," he said. "The divers are a secretive bunch."

Kormak finished his drink and left.

***

He strolled along the pier, listening to men talk. It was not all deep sea sailors in the harbour. There were fishermen and lobstermen all with small boats tied to the jetties. He passed giant ocean-going traders, and sleek war triremes and every size and class in between. He sought for the recognisable lines of the Ocean's Blade but did not see her.

He ducked into a supplier's shop and bought a spyglass and headed out to the end of the pier. He adjusted the viewfinder until eventually he saw the Ocean's Blade moored out by one of the furthest islands, near the mouth of the harbour. There seemed to be a skeleton crew on board. He shifted his point of view to the mansion. It sat on a rock and seemed to take up all the space. The walls looked thick enough to resist a siege. The only obvious way on or off the island was via the pier to which the Ocean's Blade was lashed.

A few sailors came and went from ship to mansion but most of the local ships gave the place a wide berth. Kormak studied it. He supposed that you could get in via the pier but it was always guarded and it looked like a difficult place to fight your way into. It might go better if he took a ship out and scaled the islands low cliffs and then the walls of the mansion. There were windows there that looked as if they could be forced.

He considered the approaches. He could hire a small boat to take him there but there was no guarantee that any of the locals would not betray him and raise the alarm. He supposed he could always steal a small vessel. It was not the best way to go about such a thing—without a floor plan of the building he would need to find his own way through and improvise. He'd done such things before but it wasn't the easiest way.

He studied the palace for most of the afternoon. As the day wore on, he became aware that a tall spare figure wrapped in a dark cowled cloak was watching him. The individual seemed to be looking out to sea but occasionally the head would turn in Kormak's direction and then look away again.

As the sun set, Kormak decided it was time to meet Jonas. He turned and walked down the dock. After a few moments, the cowled figure did the same. He padded up the gentle slope away from the harbour.

The taverns were doing a roaring business. The streets were full of brawling, drunken sailors, walking barefoot through the mud. Behind him, the cowled figure threaded its way through the crowd.

There was no sense in leading his pursuer to the rendezvous with Jonas. The figure appeared to be alone, so he ducked down a side alley and waited. The cloaked stranger paused at the entrance of the alley and peered into the darkness. It waited for a few moments, glanced sideways and then moved into the alley, still leaning on its staff.

Kormak stepped forward with his hand on the hilt of his weapon and said, "Why are you following me?"

"I was curious as to why someone else would be interested in the Kraken's island." The stranger's voice was high and light. The eyes caught and reflected the distant light in an odd way.

"Let me have a look at your face," Kormak said.

The figure shrugged back the cowl, revealing the face of beautiful woman. Her silver hair was cropped short. Her eyes were an odd shade of green. A milky film gave the appearance of blindness then it vanished and her eyes looked normal.

"Satisfied?" the woman asked. Her neck looked as if there were two long scars running part of its length on either side.

"Who are you?"

"You're not very polite."

"And you are surprisingly unafraid for a woman confronted by an armed man in a back alley."

She smiled. "I am armed and unlike you I can use this weapon in a heartbeat."

"You are assuming I cannot."

"A master swordsman, eh?"

"Yes," he said.

"I've killed a few of those in my time."

"With a staff? In this limited space."

Her thumb moved slightly. A long silver blade emerged from the tip of the staff, turning it into a very sharp spear. "A staff is a formidable enough weapon in the right hands," she said. "But a harpoon is even more so."

"It seems we have reached an impasse."

"No. I have a weapon drawn and you don't. I would say you are at a distinct disadvantage."

Kormak shrugged. Her smile widened. Her teeth were very white and pointed.

"You adopt a convincing air of nonchalance," she said. "I would prefer not to test your claims by spilling your blood, so perhaps we can come to an accommodation."

"If you tell me why you were studying both me and the Kraken's palace."

"Are you his guardian then?" She placed an odd emphasis on the word guardian.

"No, I am just curious about your interest."

"Ah, now I can tell you are not a local," she said, a faint mocking tone in her voice. Kormak briefly wondered what had given him away but he could see how she had come to that conclusion. Clearly she expected to be recognised and her relationship with the Kraken was apparently a well-known thing.

"I am an Aquilean."

"Yes," she said, "I know. And those are rare enough in Port Blood that I might be expected to recognise one. Yours are not a sea-faring people."

"Apparently not," he said.

"Why don't you tell me the truth," she said. "It would spare us both a lot of bother." She leaned towards him with the harpoon point.

Kormak's hand slapped the blade to one side, just behind the point. He moved forward, keeping his weight against the shaft so she could not swing it back. She dropped the blade and stepped back, drawing her dagger.

"I would not have thought that possible if I had not seen it with my own eyes," she said.

"And thus the balance of power is restored."

"I still have a dagger," she said. She did not sound so confident now.

"And I still have a sword."

"I notice you have not drawn it."

"I was taught never to draw the weapon unless I intended to kill."

"That is somewhat reassuring," she said. "Although it bespeaks an overconfidence bordering on the insane."

"Why were you watching me?"

"We have an acquaintance in common, you and I, as well as an enemy."

"And who would that be?" Kormak asked.

"The acquaintance is a Siderean priest who goes by the name of Jonas. The enemy is the man whose palace you studied so intently. Would you care for a drink?"

Kormak considered her words. It was possible that she was one of the Frater's contacts here. It was one way she would know his name. The other was that Jonas had been taken by the pirates and given up his name and description but that did not feel right. Port Blood was not a place for subtle traps.

Keeping his eyes on her, Kormak bent down and picked up her spear. His finger's found the concealed catch and he flipped it. The blade slipped back into its hiding place. He handed her the weapon and indicated she should precede him out of the alley.

"Lead on," he said.

***

She led him into a tavern near the docks. A few men called out to her as they entered. A few men looked at him with a mixture of curiosity and envy. "Good evening, captain," said the barman as she headed to a table in a distant corner.

"Captain?" Kormak said as he took a seat opposite her. She had shrugged off her cloak now. She wore a leather vest that left her arms exposed. They were long lean and muscular. She flexed her fingers. There was a faint trace of webbing between them.

"A courtesy title," she said. "I own a ship therefore I am a captain. And no, in case you are wondering I am not a reaver. I am a diver."

"A diver? One of those who seeks artefacts from the Sunken Kingdoms."

"I don't just seek them," she said. "I find them. My name is Rhiana."

"Kormak," he said. "You are one of the Seafolk."

"A true born child of Saa-Aquor."

She looked very thoughtful then added. "You sound like a priest."

"I am, as you have no doubt been told, a Guardian of the Order of the Dawn," he said. "What is your connection with Jonas?"

"In the past both his patron and his Order were clients of mine. They bought things I brought up from the Sunken Kingdoms. These days we have a mutual enemy."

There was no mistaking the glint in her eye or the malice in her voice.

"The Kraken? Why do you hate him?"

"He killed my sister Mika. She refused to sell him something he wanted. It belonged to me. He has it now."

"What does he have?"

"A relic of the Sunken Kingdoms, found in the drowned ruins of Quama Rhi. A spell-engine of considerable value to the right person, a thing perhaps unique in the world today."

"Could you be more specific?"

"A battle suit for making war beneath the ocean."

"Functioning?"

"It could be made to work by an artificer of sufficient skill. Mika was such a one. He killed her in her shop, while I was at sea, and he took the engine. She was the only kin I had left."

"I have seen him wearing it," Kormak said. "The armour is the work of the Old Ones. It looks like living flesh moulded to the wearer's body.

"No," she said, "it is metal, perhaps of Solari manufacture."

"That is not what I saw him in."

Her eyes narrowed. "You are sure?"

"Never more so".

"Perhaps he has found something better. No matter. He still owes me for what he took. You are an Aquilean. You know what a blood-debt means."

"Blood for blood, death for death."

"Yes."

"I had not heard the Seafolk went in for such things."

"I am inaugurating a new tradition."

"The Kraken has allies."

"The Quan. There is ancient hatred between such of them as survive, and my people."

"I had thought them all gone from the world. The great library at Aethelas claims that to be the case."

"Not all of them—some of the monsters still exist in the deeps. My people hunt them when they find them. They return the favour."

"What is the connection between the Kraken and the Quan?"

"I don't know. For years he sought any relic of the Quan or any book that contained the faintest hint of knowledge concerning them. He was obsessed. He quizzed both Mika and I about what we knew of the Quan, paid well for the knowledge."

"And what do you know of them?"

"They are vampires of a most peculiar sort."

"Vampires?"

"They drink the lives and the souls of their victims. Take their memories too."

Kormak thought of his encounter with the Stealer of Flesh, Razhak. "I have had experience of such."

"Yes, judging by your expression I can see you have. During the dark of the moon, for the past several months the Kraken has fed the Quan victims. Some of them were my friends."

It was exactly the sort of dark sorcery he was sworn to stop. "I can see why you hate him."

"Can you?" Rhiana sounded amused. "You look like the sort of man who seeks vengeance. I never thought I was the sort of woman. I find myself uncomfortable with hating someone so intensely. I wish to put an end to the person and thus the hate."

"I don't think it works that way," said Kormak. "What is lost is always still lost. You can't ever get it back."

She shrugged. "Nonetheless I am compelled to seek satisfaction in this matter. That is why I passed on the information I did to Jonas and his friends. I have never seen myself as a spy either."

"It seems to me that the Kraken is well protected."

"Better than you perhaps think. The Quan guard the waters around his island. They have done so since he returned from a long voyage last year. They come and go from the mansion by night. There is a deep well deep in the Kraken's house where he communes with them and they bring him dark knowledge."

"How do you know this?"

"I know the Quan hunt the waters for I have seen them. There is an underwater entrance to the mansion—I have scouted it."

"Despite the presence of the Quan."

"I do not fear them. I am not without sorcery myself." She reached out and touched his hand. A frown knitted her brow as she concentrated. The amulet against his breast grew warm.

"Either your mind is a blank or you are protected by powerful wards."

"I would advise you not to do that again. I might see it in an unfriendly light," Kormak said. "I do not like people trying to work magic on me."

"You felt something then?"

"Yes." He thought it best not to explain the nature of his defences or how he had divined what she was doing.

"I meant no harm. I merely wished to demonstrate to you why I do not fear the lurkers in the deep."

"And how do you know what goes on within the palace?"

"There are girls who visit with his crew. They must be paid ten times the normal amount to do so but there are always some who want the gold. When drunk the crew sometimes talk to them. When the girls are drunk they sometimes talk to me."

"You believe we should work together against the Kraken."

She smiled. "Unless I miss my guess, you will try to kill him anyway, and I am not about to be robbed of my vengeance. It would be best if we did not work at cross-purposes."

"I agree."

"Good," she said. She sounded pleased.

"I have business elsewhere," said Kormak. "But I propose we meet here again before the tenth bell."

"As you say."

CHAPTER FOURTEEN

KORMAK RETURNED TO the inn they had used the night before. Frater Jonas was there, nervous at being on his own in a city full of pirates.

"Sir...I mean Kormak, I am pleased to see you," said Jonas. He sounded sincere. Given the way two hard looking men at the next table stared at them, Kormak could understand why. He met their glances and held them till they looked away.

"Did your business go well," said Kormak. He spoke in a low murmur now so that no one could overhear. Judging by the amount of drinking going on that was not very likely but you never knew who might be a spy. Plenty of other whispered conversations were taking place so no one would think it at all unusual.

Jonas nodded.

"I ran into someone who claimed to know you. Her name was Rhiana."

"She found you then? She said she would seek you out down by the docks. I told her not to, but she can be stubborn."

"Next time let me know when you're going to put someone on my trail. I might have killed her."

"I did not know that I would find her so quickly or that she would seek you out. Otherwise I would have. My apologies if I caused you any problems."

"What else did you do? Did you find out anything about the Kraken?"

"He is having his ship made ready for a long voyage even though he's only just returned. His crew are a tight-lipped bunch but from what my sources have heard it looks like they won't be heading back towards the mainland."

"No more raiding then."

"Apparently so—it looks like he's preparing to head westwards out into the wild ocean over the Sunken Kingdoms. As he did last year. Have you come to any decisions yourself?"

"The Kraken is in his place of power. He has a crew of warriors, a sea filled with squid-demons and other defences in place. Our options appear to be to either catch him here or wait until he goes to sea again and overhaul him there. You will remember how that went last time."

"So you are determined to make the attempt on his life here."

"It seems like the best place."

"And you do feel this merwoman, Rhiana, can help you?"

"She can survive well enough in a sea full of Quan to scout his palace. She has some of the sorcerous gifts of her people."

"And you trust her?"

"I will work with her if our goals are the same."

"My people have had dealings with her for many years. Her information has always been first rate."

"Did you pick up any more nuggets of intelligence?"

"The Kraken is not liked here. He has many enemies but all are afraid of him. If he puts a curse on a man's ship, that ship does not return."

"I think we both understand how that works."

"His crew are a loyal and closed mouthed lot. Most of them seem to be old family retainers. Those who are not have served many years under his command."

"Old family retainers? Of the mother?"

"Yes."

"Where is she?"

"No one knows. No one even knows whether she is alive or dead. She would be an old woman if she were alive today."

"We'd best go. I arranged to meet your ally down by the docks."

***

Rhiana waited in the harbourside tavern. Around her lounged a group of tough looking men. "My crew," she said as Kormak walked over to the table.

"My associate, Jonas," Kormak said, just in case Rhiana did not want her crew to know of the connection or in case any outsider was listening in.

"He does not look like a warrior," said a large villainous looking sailor.

"He's a scholar," Kormak said. "His head is full of interesting lore."

"Good," said Rhiana. "We shall have something to talk about once this night's work is done."

"This night?" Jonas said.

Rhiana moved closer to Kormak and spoke very softly. "The tides are right. Clouds cover the moon. We can get close enough to the Kraken's palace without being spotted."

Kormak tilted his head to one side and studied the merwoman. "This is all a bit sudden," he said.

"I've been planning it for weeks," she said. "You don't have to come if you are afraid."

A taunting note sounded in her voice. Well-acquainted with the ways people could be manipulated by questioning their courage, he said, "I am not afraid."

Suspicions flickered through his mind. Did he really want to get on a ship on the harbour with this band of cutthroats? Did he really want to get into the water with a merwoman where the advantages would all be with her? Still, if it worked, this would be his best chance to get into the palace of the Kraken.

"Good," said Rhiana. She swigged back her drink, turned to her crew and said, "Let's be off."

***

The dark water rippled in their wake. The sailors sculled the small craft. Frater Jonas stood in Kormak's shadow, hand toying with the Elder Sign at his throat, clearly wondering about the wisdom of being here. Rhiana kept her gaze fixed on the Kraken's distant palace. She licked her lips. Perhaps she was more nervous than she appeared. There were two ships tied up by the island's docks. One of them was the Ocean's Blade. The other was a much larger, sailing ship, closer in design to the Sea Dragon but even more rugged looking.

He pointed it out.

"The Kraken's Reach," Rhiana said. "His flagship. His pride and joy. If I get the chance I am going to send it to the bottom of the ocean."

Her head moved from side to side and he realised that she was not studying the palace so much as the surrounding waters. Her strange eyes reflected the smallest fragments of light. Kormak realised that she could see better than he in the darkness.

"The Quan stay clear of the palace for a few hours during the dark of the moon," she said. "They go somewhere, perhaps to perform their own strange rites."

"You have been studying this place," Kormak said.

"Oh yes," she said. "And tonight I intend to make that study pay off. You'd best strip."

He did as she said. Soon he was wearing only his loincloth, his amulets and his weapons. Rhiana looked at him and said, "You have the tattoo, just as you are supposed to."

Kormak strapped the blade back onto his back. One of the sailors handed him a pot of grease. To Kormak's surprise Jonas took it, sniffed it then passed it on.

"It will keep out the cold," said Rhiana. "We're going to be in the water for some time."

"Just so long as it does not draw sharks," Kormak said.

"Is that what your friend was checking for?" Rhiana asked.

"Something like that," Jonas replied.

"There's so little trust in the world," said Rhiana. She took off her cloak and jumped into the water. Her fingers splayed and the webs between them and her toes became visible. She disappeared below the waves and did not come up.

Jonas clapped Kormak on the back and said, "Good luck." He seemed nervous about being left on the ship on his own. He was nervous about everything and yet he kept putting himself in the way of danger.

"And you," said Kormak. He dived over the side. Cold dark water closed over his head.

***

It took moments for Kormak's eyes to adjust. He was a strong swimmer and had been ever since his boyhood amid the lakes of Aquilea but this was nerve-wracking. It was dark and there were monsters in the water. On land, he would not have been troubled. He had spent his life fighting against the Old Ones and their creatures, but he was out of his element, slow, weighed down by his weapons and unable to breathe.

A figure flashed near him and his heart leapt. It was Rhiana, moving through the water with the ease of a fish, her webbed fingers and toes letting her move with a freedom that he would never be able to emulate. She tugged at his arm and pointed. He swam in that direction, wondering how much longer he would be able to hold his breath.

Her hand touched his shoulder, oddly warm in the cold water. She pushed him to one side. He resisted the impulse to struggle and saw where she was guiding him. Ahead a rock wall loomed. In it gaped a darker opening.

Rhiana produced a small pearl from within her tunic. It began to emit a faint greenish glow the colour of seaweed. The light revealed the mouth of a long dark tunnel.

The long slits in Rhiana's neck pulsed. They were gills that allowed her to breathe under water. She looked at home in a way she had never seemed on land. It was the difference between a bird on a branch and a bird in flight.

She tapped him on the shoulder again and indicated the way they needed to go. Already his lungs hurt. If he did not breathe soon he would die. His heart hammered against his ribs. His chest felt tight. Faint streams of bubbles came from his nostrils.

Sleek as seal, Rhiana entered the tunnel and vanished ahead. He followed her into the murk, wondering what would happen if they encountered one of the Quan in these depths. Rhiana might have nothing to fear in such an encounter but he would be at a definite disadvantage.

The tunnel narrowed and he remembered that the Quan had seemed boneless. Their form was elastic and would have no difficulty compressing into a narrow space. He did not have that luxury. He forced himself to swim on.

His hands grazed rock as he pulled himself through the water. The tunnel grew narrower.

It went dark. Had something happened to Rhiana? He banged into something and scrabbled against stone. He felt a wall. Was this a dead end? Had Rhiana fallen into a trap?

He could not orientate himself. He did not know which way led back and he could not find his way to the surface in the darkness. Pure stark terror filled his mind.

He was going to drown.

His heart hammered against his ribs. He felt nauseous. Vomiting here would be fatal. Be calm, he told himself. He fought down the urge to perform the breathing exercises his training in the warrior's court on Mount Aethelas had made almost instinctive.

He tried to make his mind a blank while his fingers sought for a way out. He found another opening. The tunnel had twisted upwards.

His lungs were on fire. Faint silver stars sparkled in his field of vision. Why had Rhiana not warned him of this—did she just not realise that a normal man would struggle in the tunnel. He pushed himself round the bend, scrambling in the dark, ahead now he saw a light again.

He forced himself to go on. His lungs screamed for air. He wanted more than anything just to take a deep breath. One more stroke he told himself. Just one more. He moved his arms. Another stroke. He swam up towards the light.

All thoughts except keeping going vanished from his mind.

One more stroke. Another. Don't breathe.

His head broke the surface of the water. He took in a long gulp of air and fought off a wave of dizziness.

Rhiana turned back to look at him. Water dripped from her body where she had pulled herself from the water. She studied their surroundings by the light of the gem.

He was going to ask her why she had not waited then he realised that what had seemed like hours to him could not have been more than a minute. If it had been any more he would most likely have been dead.

She reached down and he took her hand. She pulled him out of the water without effort.

They stood in a cave. Water dripped from the ceiling into the pool about ten strides across. A faint luminescent slime clung to the walls. A familiar fishy scent hung in the air. "Quan," Kormak said.

Rhiana nodded. "This is where he feeds them and comes to sport with them."

"Let us be about our business," Kormak said. He wanted to put distance between himself and that dark pool.

CHAPTER FIFTEEN

DRIPPING WET THEY made their way up a long winding corridor. The slimy walls held the smell of Quan. Manacles hung against the walls and ancient-looking mummies hung from the chains.

They followed a flight of steps leading up and stepped out. Lanterns threw their soft glow along the walkway. From ahead came the sound of men feasting and singing. The noise made it clear there was at least several score of them. Kormak padded away from the sounds of merrymaking and found another flight of stairs going up.

The banisters looked to be of the same sort found running round the decks of a man of war. The wood was antique oak, from ships timbers. He headed up the stairs while Rhiana padded along behind him.

A drunken man, head wrapped in a scarf, staggered down the stairs with a scantily clad woman on each arm.

"Been for a little swim, eh? And going for a little lie down! Got the right idea, matey," he said with a wink and staggered past Rhiana. She looked up at Kormak and smiled. Kormak took a deep breath and calmed himself. He was just glad the man was too drunk to spot a stranger.

He climbed upstairs, coming out onto a landing. A number of men and women sprawled everywhere, writhing on the floor, humping their way across the balcony while others looked on and cheered.

The stairs continued on past the balcony. He followed them without anyone else noticing. They kept moving upwards until they reached the third floor of the mansion. It was quieter and better furnished. Kormak guessed they were entering the private area of the master of the house. No one else was here and given the number of drunks below that said something. Fear and respect kept them out of this area, the sort that a sorcerer or a cruel ship's master might inspire.

Rhiana's fingers touched his shoulder. She said, "We were very lucky down there."

"Let's not spit on the Sun's blessings," said Kormak.

She pushed on ahead of him down the corridor, listening at doors and then testing them as she went. The first two doors opened easily enough. The last door would not move even when she leaned her full weight against it. Kormak moved closer and his amulets began to warm against his chest. He could see the faint glow.

"Mage-locked," he said. He pushed the amulet against the wood. Light flared and the stink of ozone filled the air as the spell dissipated.

"Useful," Rhiana said. "I must get one of those some time."

"It might interfere with your ability to breath under water," Kormak said.

"Not a fair trade," she murmured. She pushed the door open and produced the glowing pearl. Its light revealed a huge chamber dominated by a massive desk. On it lay many charts. They bore a resemblance to the ones Kormak had seen back on the pirate ship in Triturek. A compass, a set of navigational dividers and a measuring line lay near them. Rhiana moved over to the map and studied it.

"It's a chart of the Quaneth Deep," she said. Her finger traced a runic mark that looked recently added. "I've not seen anything like that before."

She turned her head and noticed something else. Kormak followed her gaze. On a stand in the corner stood a strange suit of armour. All the pieces, from its bulging shoulder guards to its greaves, had a curved streamlined look. The breastplate, greaves and armlets were made of burnished orichalcum. Intricate runework spoke of powerful magic etched into the chestplate. The helmet looked as if it would cover the whole head. The visor was made from translucent crystal. The part that covered the mouth and jaw was made from metal and connected to the back part of the chestplate by flexible tubes. Rhiana gave a small gasp, and then smiled coldly.

"What is it?" Kormak asked.

"My property. The suit of armour from the Sunken Kingdoms I told you about." She touched the runes on the chestplate and Kormak felt a brief surge of magic through his amulet. She glanced at Kormak then back at the armour again. "Put it on," she said. "It works."

"Why?" he asked.

"It will make getting out of here a lot easier."

"In what way?"

"Trust me," she said. "We don't have time to wait around here discussing things."

"No," Kormak said. "My amulets will interfere with any magic in the suit and I am not taking them off. If you're so keen to get your property out wear it yourself."

"I don't need it. You do."

"Not here. Not now."

She shrugged, tore down one of the curtains from the wall, tipped the suit from its stand and then wrapped it clinking in the cloth. "You're not going to make things easy, are you?" she said.

"Not when I don't understand what is happening."

"No doubt such caution has kept you alive in the past," she said, with a note of irony. "You are prepared to break into a fortified mansion to kill a man but you will not risk putting on a suit of armour which will aid you."

"I do not play with magic unless I am forced to."

"A wise choice," said a voice Kormak had heard before. He glanced around. The Kraken stood in the doorway, the alien armour still grafted to his body. The Teardrop of Leviathan glittered on his chest. The ruby on the Kraken's ring finger reflected its light. In his right hand he held a short metal rod. "I confess I had not expected to see you again, not here anyway. And certainly not so soon."

"How did you know we were here?" Rhiana asked.

"You disrupted the warding spell on my chamber. I sensed it as I would sense the ending of any spell I had cast."

Rhiana glared at him. "This is mine. You stole it from me and my sister."

"I needed it. She refused to accept a more than fair price. I would not let her stubbornness stand in the way of my destiny. You may have it back now if you wish. It has served its purpose. I have something better." His long hand, gloved in the same black chitin as his armour, indicated his chest.

There was something in the man's unblinking stare that told Kormak that he really believed what he said. The Kraken was not sane as other men measured sanity.

"Just like that?" Rhiana said. "We can take the armour and go and you will just let us."

"I'll let you go. Why not? I am not your enemy. You had something I once needed. If your sister had been less stubborn she would not have died."

He turned, looked at Kormak and said, "You, on the other hand, are a problem. I have no wish to fight with the Order of the Dawn but I suspect they won't give me much choice in the matter. You do represent that rather fearsome bunch of fanatics, don't you? The sword gives it away."

Kormak nodded and took a slow step closer. "You have practised dark sorcery. You have consorted with demons."

"The Quan are not demons."

"They are as close to it as makes no difference."

"I would expect someone like you to see things that way."

Kormak edged closer. "Why did you need her artefact armour? Why did you kill her sister?"

The Kraken's eyes followed Kormak's gaze. The corners of his mouth turned up in the faintest hint of a mocking smile. "I needed it to find and make contact with the Quan in the deeps that they haunt. And to find certain objects long lost in the depths of the World Ocean."

He gestured to the living breastplate enclosing his chest. "I do not need it any more. The Quan have provided me with this. It belonged to Dhagoth himself. It lets me communicate with them more effectively, among other things."

He glanced towards Rhiana. "You should thank me. I have made that armour functional once more. I have increased its value by a factor of ten."

His spoke in a reasonable tone, as if they had all met in an office to discuss polite business. The cold, unblinking eyes flickered back towards Kormak as he took another step closer. The predatory smile widened a little. Kormak wondered why the sorcerer had made no attempt to call his guards. Was he really so confident? Kormak could not help but feel he was falling into a trap.

He took another step. "Why did you take the gem from the Triurids?"

"Is this to be an inquisition then, Guardian?"

"I am curious."

"I am afraid I must keep the secret of the Teardrop of Leviathan to myself for a bit longer but rest assured the world will soon learn why. It is the key to my rightful kingdom."

"I think King Aemon would disagree with you." Kormak took another step.

The Kraken's eyes narrowed and his mouth became a flat tight line at the mention of the king's name. Pure hatred glittered in his eyes. "I don't believe my brother has any say in the matter. And believe me, I will make a better king than he ever was."

Once again there was the same sense of utter belief in the Kraken's voice, a confidence that brooked no argument.

"You will never be king of anywhere," said Rhiana. "You will pay for blood with blood."

She advanced and for a moment the Kraken's attention focused on her.

Kormak whipped his blade from the scabbard and moved towards the Kraken. Cat-quick, the sorcerer lifted the metal rod and parried the blow. Electric agony surged up Kormak's arm, spasming his muscles. Stars flickered before his eyes. The smell of ozone filled the air. He had thought himself protected against magic but clearly this energy was not sorcerous. This was like being hit by a trapped thunderbolt.

Rhiana whipped back her arm and cast her harpoon-staff. It flashed through the air towards the Kraken. He stepped aside and the blade buried itself in the wall. With enormous effort Kormak forced himself to his feet. The Kraken's eyes widened and he seemed to suddenly become aware of the danger he was in. He dived back through the door, shouting for aid. The armour gave his movement an inhuman sinister quality.

Rhiana leaned down and helped Kormak up, supporting him with one hand, while she held the package containing the armour in the other. With enormous effort, he stretched out his fingers and grasped the hilt of his dropped blade. He was not going to lose it now.

Feet thundered up the stairs. Rhiana tottered into the corridor. The sorcerer was nowhere to be seen. He would not need to fight himself when his men could do the killing and dying for him.

Rhiana pulled Kormak along towards the top of the stairs while he tried to regain control of his limbs. He reeled like a drunken sailor on a spree. A group of pirates appeared at the head of the stair. Rhiana whirled the bundled armour at their leader, catching him on the head with it. The man toppled and she leapt among them, striking left and right at them. A pirate fell with each blow, but they soon overcame their surprise and they had weapons and she did not.

Kormak half-fell into their midst, striking out clumsily with his sword. His razor sharp blade cut flesh and drew blood. In the half-light the confused pirates did not quite understand what was happening.

Control returned to his limbs. He began to move with his customary smoothness, cutting a crimson swathe down to the second landing. Soon he bled from a dozen small cuts. They stung more and more as the numbing effect of the Kraken's magic wore off.

Behind him, Rhiana had picked up a cutlass and strode down the steps, striking anyone who seemed about to get behind Kormak.

Shouts echoed through the mansion. The pirates might be drunk but the prospect of battle had a sobering effect and sheer weight of numbers would be enough to pull them down in the end.

The Kraken's men raced towards them as they reached the bottom of the stairwell. Kormak stepped to one side to let them pass, shouting, "Quickly! Someone tried to kill the captain."

The drunken pirates met their comrades on the stair. Weapons clashed as fights broke out. Kormak knew the confusion would not last for long. He grabbed Rhiana by the hand and led her along the corridor in the direction of the entrance to the cellars.

Moments later they were racing downwards through the damp corridors. They slammed the door behind them and wedged it shut with Rhiana's dagger. Kormak's heart sank. He realised that the only way out was through the long water-filled tunnel and that the Quan might be waiting for them when they entered it.

CHAPTER SIXTEEN

KORMAK GAZED AT the dark shimmering surface of the pool. Rhiana stood at the edge, the bundle still on her arm. She studied Kormak with a critical eye. "Those cuts will need to be seen to. They may well attract sharks and other things once we are in the water."

"We don't have anything to bind so many wounds and we wouldn't have the time to do so even if we did."

"There's another way," she said. "You could get into the armour. It will trap any blood until we get back to the boat."

"You're determined to get me into it."

"I would wear it myself but I don't need it and I am not bleeding like a butchered steer."

Kormak took a deep breath and contemplated the pool once. The sound of fists battering against the door echoed down the corridor. It would not take long for the pirates to break through.

"What exactly will this armour do for me?"

"It should provide you with air while you're under water. It may also help you move. I suspect that Elder Sign will cause problems though."

"I am not taking it off," said Kormak.

"At least put the armour on."

Kormak nodded. She unrolled the bundle and helped him into armour. The limbs of the suit were made from scaled metal, thin and flexible as cloth. It was heavy and cold as a suit of plate mail when he donned it. A strange tingling began as Rhiana's fingers passed over the runes of the chestplate. The amulets on his chest heated. Crackling sounded in his ears.

Rhiana looked grim. "It's not going to work properly while you wear that damn Elder Sign," she said.

Behind them came the sound of shattering wood and howling voices. Splinters flew as men hacked at the door with blades.

"Well," she said. "Too late to worry about things now. Unless you are keen to make a heroic last stand against an entire ship's crew, I suggest we take our leave."

She dived headlong into the water. Kormak stood for a moment, looked at the pool and then back to the entrance through which the pirates would come. Waiting here and getting himself killed would do no one any good. He jumped into the water.

Darkness rippled over his head. Rhiana's glowing pearl lit the way into the narrow tunnel. He shuddered at the thought of passing back through it in the bulky armour. He cursed the merwoman for persuading him to don it.

The suit grew warmer but it did seem easier to move in once he was immersed. It flowed naturally with his movements. The crystalline visor made it easier for him to see in the gloom. The weight did not drag him down. Magic was at work here.

He did not dare to breathe.

Rhiana beckoned for him to follow and then swam on ahead. He followed her into the long dark tunnel. It seemed even more claustrophobic now that he wore the armour.

He forced himself through the gap, wriggling more than swimming. The crystal of the helmet grated against the stone, but the translucent material did not chip or shatter.

He kept moving. He was tired from the effort of fighting. His lungs were going to burst. His amulet grew hotter against his chest. He caught the smell of ozone within the suit.

He came to the bend in the tunnel but this time he was ready. He squirmed around and kicked out with his feet so that they hit the stone of the wall and propelled him forward. The impact jarred his whole body.

The greenish glow of the pearl lit the way ahead. His scabbarded sword dragged along the ceiling of the tunnel, slowing him.

Weariness and pain were taking their toll. His lungs felt as if they were going to explode if he did not take a breath.

The air left an acrid chemical taint on his tongue. He took another gulp, not sure what would happen once he had exhausted the air in the crystal helmet. He had heard of miners choking to death on bad vapours deep underground. Perhaps this would happen to him.

He pushed on along the tunnel and out into the dark waters of the harbour. Ahead, Rhiana swam up towards a dark shadow that could only be their boat. Beneath him he thought he saw other dark shadows, heading upwards.

What were they? Sharks? Quan?

He pulled for the surface as strongly as he could, not wanting to be caught by anything large rising in these cold dark waters. Dizziness assaulted him. His breath emerged in ragged gasps. The Elder Sign burned against his chest.

He forced himself to keep swimming, moving upwards until his head broke the surface. He clawed at the seal of the helmet, trying to find the clasp, afraid that he would drown in the poisonous vapours while all around clean air blew past him on the harbour winds.

Nearby a dark fin broke the water's surface and began to move towards him. He kept going towards the side of the ship, praying to the invisible sun that he would reach it before the fin reached him.

Rhiana pulled herself over the side of the small craft. The crew and Jonas greeted her.

He grew dizzier and dizzier. He considered stopping and drawing his sword. The open water between him and the boat looked like a short distance but at his swimming speed it might as well be the length of the harbour.

The boat came closer. The fin was closer still when he looked over his shoulder.

He emptied his mind, ignored his aching muscles and lungs, took one more stroke and then another. He reached the wooden side of the little craft. Rhiana reached over to pull him aboard. Other hands reached down to help.

Something touched his leg, pushing him up from below, out of the water and into the boat. He flopped down onto the wooden boards. Rhiana reached down and unhooked the helmet. He drank in the clean air. He luxuriated in the salty tang, the stink of the harbour, the distant blazing lights, the feeling of still being alive.

The shark had not attacked him.

Something heavy splashed. Droplets of water landed on his face, showering over all the sailors. A weird honking noise sounded. A sleek, finned shape flipped itself through the air and returned to the water.

He realised he had made a mistake. The fin belonged to a dolphin, not a shark.

He pulled himself upright and looked out at the lights of the Kraken's palace. Men swarmed the walls now, carrying lanterns and torches. More pirates, brandishing swords, raced along the jetties to the moored boats. It was only a matter of time before they spotted Rhiana's small craft.

"Get us out of here," Rhiana said, her voice little more than a whisper. "Row. And someone give me a hand with the Guardian's wounds."

Without waiting for another word, the sailors began to pull towards the distant line of warehouses.

***

The tavern was brightly lit even this late at night. The sailors seemed happy. Rhiana had stowed the armour they had taken away in an oilskin wrap. The unguent Jonas had applied to Kormak's wounds dulled their pain. Kormak was happy to be dressed once more in his tunic and britches. He longed for the reassurance of wearing his old armour. It had been a long and nerve-wracking night.

Jonas sipped at his wine and cast his glance between Kormak and the diver captain. "Well," he said at last, "Did you get him?"

"He escaped us," said Rhiana. "But we did at least reclaim my property."

"That is a great consolation," said Jonas. Irony dripped from his tone.

Kormak remained silent. Anything he said would sound like an excuse for failure, and with good reason. He had failed. The Kraken lived and could still go about whatever schemes he had devised. Worse than that, he knew that Kormak hunted him. He had lost the vital element of surprise. His target would take counter-measures. In this city, those might prove to be formidable. The Kraken was a captain as well as a sorcerer, and he was rich. He would be able to find powerful allies.

"It might be more useful than you think," said Rhiana, unabashed by Jonas's tone. "When properly configured that armour will let a man dive to the very bottom of the ocean."

"Why would we need to do that?" Jonas asked.

"Wrong question," Rhiana replied. "You should be asking why the Kraken needed to do that."

"And I suppose you have an answer," the priest said.

"He needed it to make contact with the Quan. They appeared about a month after he took the suit. The timing would be about right."

"Fascinating," said Jonas, in a manner that suggested his patience was wearing thin.

"And I learned something else. I saw the charts he was looking at. I know where he is heading."

"Please don't keep us in suspense, my lady," said Jonas.

"He's heading out to the Quaneth Deep.

"And what will he find there?"

"It's not a place anybody goes, not even divers."

"So you don't know?" Jonas said.

"It is shunned for a reason. There are dark rumours about the place. It is right on the edge of the Sunken Kingdoms and the seabed there falls off steep as a cliff and maybe deep as a mountain is tall. The sea there is blighted and that blighting seems to rise out of the depths."

Jonas gave a grim smile. "I must admit it does sound like exactly the sort of place I would expect the Kraken to go, but what was he seeking there?"

"Something connected to the Quan," said Rhiana. "Legend has it they come and go from the Deep sometimes, the few of them that are left."

"He picked up the Teardrop of Leviathan in Triturek," said Kormak. "I doubt that is unconnected. Have you made any headway with those notes you collected from his ship?"

"Alas I have not had the time."

"A pity. They might have given us some clue as to what he is up to."

Jonas shrugged and said, "Well, Sir Guardian, what do you think we should do now?"

Kormak considered the options. "If worst comes to worst we should prepare ourselves for a long sea voyage," he said. "It seems that sooner or later the Kraken is going to seek the Quaneth Deeps."

Kormak looked at Rhiana. "Do you have a ship?"

"A small craft. It would be no match for the Kraken's vessel and my crew is only a fraction of the size of his."

A man entered the tavern, glanced around and made straight for the table. It was Terves garbed in a tunic and white shirt but still carrying himself with the gait of an old soldier. He made straight for the table and almost saluted when he reached Kormak.

"What are you doing here?" Jonas demanded.

Terves gave him a grim smile. "Looking for you. I've searched near every tavern in this hellhole town too."

"Where's Zamara? What happened to the Sea Dragon?"

"Best come and take a look for yourself. It will soon be light outside anyway."

CHAPTER SEVENTEEN

ZAMARA'S SHIP NO longer flew a Siderean flag. It had been hastily painted black and it flew a black flag.

Zamara was no longer dressed as a noble of the Siderean court. He wore a simple red coat with a scarf tied around his head. His marines had removed the Star and Dragon emblem of Siderea from their shields, overpainting them with scores of new patterns. They peered over the sides of the ship as if expecting it to be stormed by the pirate hordes at any moment.

"You make a convincing looking corsair," said Kormak as he surveyed the young nobleman.

Zamara gave a sour grimace. "I may have to become one in the not too distant future, if I cannot report success to His Majesty." He shot a glance at Jonas to see how the priest took this. It was clear he was not entirely joking. His eyes lighted on Rhiana and he paused for a moment then gave her a smile. She smiled back.

Jonas said, "You took the ship into some backwater and repainted her, didn't you? Shortened the masts, scuffed up the crew. A quick job of camouflage and then you came in."

"It was pointless waiting out on the sea-lanes when the man we seek is in here." He sounded convinced of that. Kormak remembered his first impressions of Zamara. The captain still sought glory. And he had no reason to return and report failure. It would cost him his head.

"Your help would have been useful last night," said Jonas.

Kormak doubted that. There were not enough marines here to have made a difference storming the fortified manor. At least now, they had a ship with which to pursue the Kraken.

Even as that thought occurred to him, he saw the long lean form of the Ocean's Blade moving away from the docks and out to sea. Her oars splashed rhythmically through the water. Zamara's eyes followed his former flagship like those of a jealous lover watching an old flame depart with a new man.

Behind the Ocean's Blade came the Kraken's Reach, more massive even than the Sea Dragon. On her sterncastle stood the familiar commanding figure of the sorcerer. He surveyed the harbour with total arrogance. He knew every eye was watching his departure and wondering where he was going.

Just for a moment, Kormak saw a black-cowled figure looking out from one of the portholes in the sterncastle. At least one Quan lurked on board.

"Get ready to haul anchor, dogs," Zamara bellowed at the crew. Kormak studied the two departing ships and did a quick head count. They pirates outnumbered them and they hunted two ships. The odds were not very good even with Rhiana's men along to bolster their numbers. They had no choice but to pursue though. The alternative was to let the Kraken get away.

Rhiana looked at Zamara. "Give me an hour. There are things we need to find."

"I am not sure I can. We might lose him."

"I know where he is going," she said. "And don't worry, we will catch him."

Zamara looked like he might disagree but Rhiana gave him a winning smile then looked at Kormak.

"We may need the armour," she said. "I'll have my men bring it."

Kormak thought about the implications of her words. Did she seriously believe they might have to pursue the Kraken down into the depths of the World Ocean?

Judging by the grim set of her jaw, she did.

***

Two hours later, the harbour of Port Blood fell away astern. A dolphin followed in their wake, leaping out of the water and then splashing back. Sailors and marines shouted encouragement at it. They considered such creatures lucky.

Kormak, Jonas and Rhiana stood on the forecastle, beside the catapult, and scanned the horizon. Behind them, on the sterncastle Zamara shouted orders to the crew. He seemed once more to be in his element.

"Our captain surprised me," said Jonas. "I would not have expected him to be so bold as to come into the harbour like that."

"He has nothing left to lose," Kormak said. "If he goes home now he can report only failure."

"Perhaps," said Jonas. "Perhaps he had something else in mind, like becoming permanently resident in Port Blood."

"He would not be the first," said Rhiana.

"You would know about such things," said Jonas.

"I am not a corsair," she said. "I am a diver."

"But you choose to live among corsairs," said Jonas.

"It's as good a place as any for one like me. It is close to the Sunken

Kingdoms and there is a ready market for what I find. And it is refreshingly free from taxmen and other thieves."

Jonas laughed. "The pirates of Port Blood impose their own taxes on everyone else."

"Not on me," she said.

"Why is that exactly?" Jonas asked.

"Unlike most seamen, they consider it lucky to have my folk about. They do not slay the Sea Children. Only the Kraken has ever done that."

Red anger blazed in her voice. Kormak recognised the underlying rage. He had felt it himself at times.

"He is certainly a man who needs to be stopped," said Jonas. "I would give a lot to know what he is up to."

"Nothing good, that is certain," said Rhiana.

"Perhaps you should get back to those coded journals," Kormak said. "They might help you find out."

Jonas nodded and strode below.

"What journals are these?" Rhiana asked.

"You'll find out soon enough I suspect," said Kormak.

***

An island rose from the sea, glittering in the sunlight. What looked at first like a hillock was an enormous head. The sharp sail-like piece of stone near it was not a towering rock but a hand. He gazed upon a gigantic statue emerging from the sea.

"The waters cannot be too deep here," Kormak said.

"You think," Rhiana replied. "Wait a few moments and you'll see."

The ship moved into the shadow of the stone colossus. The waters were clear as glass. A long way below the ruins of a great city covered the ocean floor. They were passing over an enormous palace, rising, floor upon floor, storey upon storey upwards. On its roof stood the great statue whose head they could see.

Not a sailor cursed. Not a soldier spoke. Even Zamara said nothing. Looking down Kormak could see that the roofs of the palace had all tumbled. Shoals of fish swam through the rubble. Long stalks of seaweed drifted above the fallen towers.

"Once there was a city bigger than Trefal down there," Jonas said. He had emerged from his cabin below to take a closer look at the prodigy.

"Bigger than Vandemar," said Kormak. "All gone now."

"The Angels spoke. The mountains burned. The sky rained fire. The earth shook. The kingdoms sank," Jonas quoted from scripture. "The sons of the Sun fled across the sea in their tall ships seeking sanctuary from the wrath of their god."

"A whole land drowned," said Kormak.

"More than one," said Rhiana.

"You have hunted among the ruins down there," Jonas said.

"Little point. A thousand divers have been doing it for twice a thousand years."

"They say the Sunken Lands were once as great as the Kingdoms of the Sun, the Kingdoms of Shadow and Ash and the Kingdoms of Snow and Ice combined. I am starting to believe that," said Jonas.

"They were certainly populous. Do you think your god really cursed them?"

Kormak could not help but notice the way she placed the emphasis on *your*. Jonas appeared to give the matter serious consideration.

"That's what the Scriptures claim," he said. "It is what the Church believes."

"Is that what you believe?" Rhiana asked.

"There are other documents and other sources," said Jonas, keeping his voice low, as if he spoke of matters he did not want anybody else to overhear. "The Seleneans claim that it was war between the Old Ones and their foes triggered the catastrophe."

"I spoke to an Old One who claimed they used weapons so terrible that the continents themselves were shattered," Kormak said.

"Do you think it true?" Jonas asked.

Kormak shrugged. "Another said it was the Children of the Sun themselves who were responsible. They used too much magic, disrupted the leylines that kept the continent above the waves. It could have been any of these explanations or none. We are unlikely to ever find out."

"And you don't care?" Jonas said. There was an accusing note in his voice, as if he could not understand how anyone could feel that way.

"I am interested," said Kormak. "But I am not going to lose any sleep over the fact that I don't know."

"I have had nightmares about it sometimes," the priest said. "They say when the Islands of the Sun sank, waves as high as mountains battered the land, that Leviathan rose from the deep, that millions upon millions died."

"I have had similar dreams," said Rhiana. She sounded thoughtful. "I wonder if they are memories of reality."

Jonas said, "We know the Solari emerged from the Sea on the wings of the storm to conquer the lands the Old Ones ruled. We know that their cities sank. We have just seen evidence of it. It was some part of reality."

They fell silent. The waters darkened again and the drowned city faded from view. Kormak suspected they were all glad of it.

***

Days later, Jonas came flying out onto the deck waving the sheaf of papers he had found back in Triturek. "I have cracked it," he said. There was excitement and terror in his voice. "I have broken the code."

"Are you sure?" Kormak asked.

"It was simple once I puzzled it out. The cypher is an ancient Selenean numerological one. It was the language confused me. I was expecting either modern Sunlander, Solari or the Old Tongue. One of those is what any civilised man ought to have used."

"I take it the Kraken did not."

Jonas shook his head. "He cyphered it in the Low Dialect of Skorpean."

"The slaver's tongue."

"Indeed. The Kraken spent time there as a youth, dealing in flesh. I would have seen it sooner but the spelling of the words is to, say the least, non-standard and the grammar, well... it was execrable."

"What did you find?" It was then that Kormak noticed how pale the priest looked and how dilated his pupils were. He looked either exalted or terrified.

"I think we should talk with the captain and Rhiana," he said. "It will save me having to repeat myself."

***

"Well?" Zamara said. His cabin looked even smaller with all four of them squeezed in. Rhiana perched beside Kormak on a drop-down bed that hung from chains on the wall. Zamara sat on his sea chest. Jonas leaned against the closed door, too excited to sit. "What is this important news you have?"

"I have decoded the Kraken's journal," Jonas said. "I know what it is he seeks. I know why he wanted the Teardrop of Leviathan."

"Why?" Kormak asked.

Jonas closed his eyes for a moment, put his hands together as if in prayer and then looked at the ceiling. He gulped in air before he spoke. "The journals go back a long way. To before the Kraken ever began his hunt for the Quan artefacts. They started with stories his mother told him of Dhagoth. The witch belonged to one of the cults that worshipped him and still offered sacrifice."

"Dhagoth is dead," said Kormak.

"So are many other Old Ones. It does not stop their cults worshipping them. Their followers believe they will return some day."

"An interesting theological point," said Zamara, "but what has this to do with the Kraken?"

"The witch taught her son more than spells. She told him about the Quan, Dhagoth's greatest servants, and about Leviathan, Dhagoth's steed. She believed that Leviathan was the mother of the Quan, not a mere monster but a living vessel who gave birth to countless children. This knowledge passed down from priestess to priestess for a hundred generations."

"My folk have similar stories," said Rhiana. "When I spoke of them to the Kraken he nodded as if he was agreeing with something he had heard before."

"I was taught the Quan were Dhagoth's children," Kormak said.

Jonas's head bobbed in brisk agreement. "So was I. But the Kraken's journal tells a different tale. Leviathan was more than a simple monster, she, for I think I need to start calling her that, was a vessel and a womb. She spawned the Quan in the thousands as fish spawn eggs. If the Kraken is to be believed Leviathan was home to them, a ship the size of a city that could swim through the deepest seas and cross the seas between the stars."

Zamara grunted. "It sounds like exactly the sort of tale to tell a child. Ships that swim between the stars—who would credit that?"

"The Kraken, for one. Dhagoth for another."

"What?"

"Dhagoth bound Leviathan when first she fell from the sky into the ocean. While she was stunned from her great fall, he drove aetherial crystals into her flesh. He siphoned her life force into the gems. The Teardrop, the master crystal, allowed him to control the great beast and all her children. He could inflict agony on her or destroy her at his whim."

"It sounds like something that one of the great Old Ones would do," said Kormak.

"Leviathan was vast, a citadel that roamed the seas and unleashed Dhagoth's armies. Its tentacles destroyed city walls. Its movement generated waves that swamped cities."

"How then was Dhagoth defeated and where is the monster now?" Zamara asked. He tried to make the words sound like a sneer but there was an undercurrent of fear in his voice.

"Now we come to the crux of the matter," said Jonas. "War erupted between the Old Ones. They had destroyed or conquered all of the other Elder Races. They had no one left to fight for dominance but each other. Tritureon and Dhagoth battled for control of the seas. Tritureon forged a harpoon made from the swords of slaughtered Angels and used it to slay Dhagoth. He ripped the master crystal from the heart of Leviathan and sent the corpse to the bottom of the Ocean."

"That's all very well," said Zamara. "But it must have happened millennia ago and has nothing to do with us."

"The Kraken believes Tritureon erred."

"And he would know better than a false god, I suppose," Zamara said.

"He believes that Leviathan was wounded almost unto death. She sank to the ocean's bottom and lies there dormant, healing in her vast slow way. A few of the Quan remain awake in the depths, watching over her, tending her wounds, preserving her flesh."

Kormak could see the way this was going. "The Kraken believes that he can waken Leviathan with the Teardrop and bind the monster using Dhagoth's spells."

Jonas nodded. "He talked with the Quan using the ancient spells his mother had taught him. He located the beast in the Quaneth Deeps. He will rouse Leviathan and this time there will be no Tritureon to stop her."

"Is it possible?" Rhiana asked. She sounded appalled.

"Who knows? But he has spent his lifetime planning this and no one knows more about Leviathan than he. If he succeeds he will be all but invincible. Leviathan could swallow fleets, smash cities, birth armies. There is nothing in this age of the world that can oppose her."

"There are other potential outcomes, that are even worse than the Kraken enslaving her," Kormak said. "He might rouse Leviathan and be unable to bind her. Think of such a beast rampaging uncontrolled along the coasts of the Sunlands. Think of armies of Quan unleashed."

"I knew I could trust you to see things at their darkest, Guardian," said Jonas. His teeth were brilliant white when he smiled but there was no mirth in his eyes.

Zamara's gaze flickered between the two of them. He was a Siderean. His nation's great cities lay on its long coastline. Its wealth came from the sea. Its empire throve on maritime trade. He had witnessed what a single Quan could do with his own eyes. "We need to stop him," he said.

"We need to kill him," said Rhiana. "And we need to make sure that his dark knowledge dies with him."

All of them nodded agreement.

Zamara laid out his charts on the desk. They were far less complete than the ones Kormak had seen back in the Kraken's palace. They showed open ocean with a scattering of islands along with warnings of whirlpools and sea monsters and other things. The fancies of the cartographers had got the better of them. They had spent more time embellishing the cartouches than making the chart.

Even the Sidereans, the greatest seafarers among the Sunlanders, had very little knowledge of this part of the ocean. The borders of the maps were so elaborate because the map-makers knew so little about the area they were illustrating.

How had the Kraken come by his charts? He doubted he would ever get the chance to find out.

"If your memory is correct, milady," Zamara said. "We should arrive over the Quaneth Deeps in less than a day. If we don't overhaul the Kraken before then."

"Or he does not summon another of his giant pets to be rid of us," said Jonas. His tone was dark. Kormak could not blame him for that. The thought of encountering another such beast so far out in the ocean was not a reassuring one.

"If we encounter the monster we will be better prepared this time." Zamara said. "We have pots of alchemical fire ready and you can bet the men in the crow's nest are keeping their eyes peeled for any disturbances. There are men beside the war-engines day and night ready to spring into action as soon as the warning is given."

Zamara was saying this as much for his own benefit as theirs. He seemed to need reassurance that all would go well.

Rhiana said, "He can only summon the monsters if there is one in the waters nearby."

"How can you be certain of that?" Zamara asked.

"When you last encountered him, he did not summon a deep dweller straight away, did he? He did not bring one in to shatter your fleet when it waited in the river mouth."

"True," Zamara said. "But there must be plenty of monsters out there now."

"No. And I will tell you when there are," Rhiana said.

"And how will you know?"

"It is a gift of mine. It has kept me alive for a long time now."

"Let's hope you stay that way," said Jonas. Rhiana gave him her ravishing smile. Clearly she was less worried about the ship going down out here than they were. That too was understandable. If worst came to worst she could swim home. The rest of them would not be so lucky.

"If we do overtake the Kraken, he has two ships to our one," Kormak said looking at the captain. "How do you intend to deal with those odds?"

"If we can we will board and retake the Ocean's Blade," Zamara said. "And then we will sink the Kraken's Reach."

"That's your plan?"

"He has no more than a skeleton crew on the galley, and we have a double compliment of warriors thanks to Captain Rhiana. My men know how to sail that galley. If we seize it, we can use it."

He sounded like what he was, a desperate man trying to convince others they had a chance.

"There is at least one Quan on the Kraken's Reach," Kormak said.

"Then we shall rely on you to kill it, Sir Kormak," said Zamara. "And the sorcerer as well."

"Does anybody have anything to add? Anything you would like to share? Now is not the time to be keeping secrets. All our lives are going to be at risk before sunset tomorrow..."

No one said anything. "Very well then," said Zamara. "You can get some sleep."

It was clear he was going to be spending the night on deck, wrapped in his cloak. He was a diligent ship's master.

CHAPTER EIGHTEEN

KORMAK STOOD ON the forecastle, looking out into the night. Something slid through the water ahead of them, riding the bow wave. He sensed the presence of Rhiana behind him, caught her faint salty scent.

"The dolphin has been with us since we left Port Blood," he said.

"How can you be sure it's the same one?"

"It is, isn't it?"

"Yes."

"It is your familiar?"

She laughed. "You think I am some sort of witch."

"I have heard it said that the Sea Folk bonded with dolphins and seals and other aquatic creatures, even whales."

"Your education covered that did it?"

"My education covered many things."

"I'll bet."

"Is it your familiar?"

"You don't give up do you?"

"It's not in my nature."

"Yes. It is my familiar. What are you going to do now? Ask the priest to burn me?"

"No."

"I thought that is what your Order did, when it wasn't bribed to leave well alone."

"My Order hunts Old Ones who break the Law. Men too, mostly wizards."

"I have heard otherwise."

"Perhaps because it sometimes is otherwise."

She came round to stand beside him. He was very aware of her nearness. Her strange eyes caught the light. At that moment she did not look very human. "My Order consists of men. Some men are weak. Some men take bribes. It does not mean that all men do."

"You exonerate your brethren so easily don't you? It's always easy for you priests."

"I am not a priest. I am a soldier."

Her mouth twisted in a faint moue of disapproval.

"You don't like priests, do you?"

"No."

"Why?"

"They don't like me. They don't like anybody who is not what they define as human."

"People are like that."

"Again, you let your people off so easily."

"I know what it is like to be an outsider," he said.

"At least they think you are human."

"I know some people who think Aquileans have horns, tails and cloven hooves."

She laughed. "Do you?"

"Only the hooves. That's why I wear boots."

"Was it part of your cunning plan to infiltrate the Order of the Dawn?"

"Yes. What's it like?"

"What's what like?"

"Being down there in the depths, swimming among the rubble of kingdoms." He was curious, as he often was about things he would never experience. It had led to some interesting conversations with Old Ones in his time.

"It's strange and it's beautiful. There are things that can stagger you with their loveliness. There are monsters that would give you nightmares. Well maybe not you, but you know what I mean. It is home for me in a way that the surface never really will be. It's funny I sometimes think I have more in common with the Quan than with you surface dwellers." She said it as if confessing to an unmentionable sin.

"They say the Old Ones made your people, just as they made the Quan."

"They did not make the Quan. In ancient days the squid folk fought with the Old Ones and lost. Dhagoth enslaved those who survived. He made them his servants and his hunters. He used them to fight his enemies. He turned their last Leviathan into his palace. At least so my people believe."

"The Old Ones did make your people though." He was not sure why he was pushing that point home. Maybe he just wanted to get some reaction, see some emotion appear in those extraordinary eyes.

"So the Elders used to claim. They took ordinary human fisher-folk and transformed them. That is why we are still blood kin to the people of the Land. We still have much in common even if the Old Ones altered our lungs to let us breathe under the sea. The Quan came from somewhere else though, a different world beyond the sky."

Kormak paused to consider the vista of the vast expanse of time and space conjured up by her words. How little they knew of the Old Ones and what they had done. They had bent entire peoples to their will before civil war brought their empire crashing down. Now all that was left were a few survivors of a race that had once been close to gods.

He thought of the gigantic statue he had seen emerging from the sea. Perhaps the same was true of his own people. Perhaps those who claimed that the world was caught in an inevitable downward spiral to chaos and destruction were correct.

"You are looking unusually thoughtful," Rhiana said.

"It happens sometimes," Kormak said. He smiled. "The fit always passes though."

"Ever the man of action, eh?"

"Yes," he said.

"I think you do yourself a disservice."

Kormak shrugged and looked into her alien eyes, wondering what was passing through her mind. "We will see action soon enough," he said.

She looked off into the distance, in the direction in which he suspected the Kraken's craft lay. "I wonder what he is up to. He has spent years planning this and as much treasure as any man could use in a normal lifetime."

"Some men desire things other than money. Some use it as a tool." He did not want to tell her what Jonas had told him about the Kraken's relationship with King Aemon. He had been given the knowledge in trust. She might have heard the Kraken talk about his brother, but he did not need to confirm any suspicions she might have.

"Or perhaps he plans on living longer than a normal lifetime. The Quan had that secret and if he becomes a lifestealer then he will have it too."

Kormak considered this. He had met many men whose ambitions had reached far beyond those of ordinary mortals. He had killed most of them.

He wondered if he would succeed this time or whether it would be his own life that ended. Every time he set out on a mission that possibility arose. The odds foretold that one day death would claim him as it had claimed other Guardians.

It came to him then that the sea made him uneasy. He did not like being confined aboard a ship. He did not like the idea that if this floating wooden platform was lost so was his life. His skill at arms would make no difference so far out of sight of land. Mortal strength would not save him. He relied on this vessel and its crew.

Their vessel was huge and strong, but he had seen seas whose waves could swallow it like a shark taking down a minnow. He thought of the Kraken and the giant squid he had summoned. If such a thing were to attack them now, it would not matter whether he could kill it. They were too far from land to ever make their way back.

"What troubles you, Sir Kormak?" Rhiana asked.

"I find I do not like the idea of spending too much time at sea," he said.

She smiled that dazzling smile. "I am the same on land. I never really feel at home there in the thin air and bright sunlight."

Her smile vanished like the moon going behind a cloud. "I fear though that this matter will be resolved beneath the water. There is no land at the spot marked on the Kraken's charts. He seeks something beneath the sea and if I read those charts aright it will be down deep. I fear that is where Leviathan lurks."

And there it was, Kormak thought. She had put her finger on what was troubling him. He had a foreboding that he was going to have to go deep beneath the waves and face the Kraken and the Quan in their own environment.

"You don't think we will overhaul him before he reaches it."

She shook her head. "Not with these winds and these currents. We will not be too far behind him though. At very least we will have the opportunity to sink his ship. Perhaps we can do it before he goes into the Deeps."

"That's something at least," Kormak said.

"If he does go below I will follow him," Rhiana said. She waited for him to say something.

"As will I," he said. "I have come this far to get him. I will go as far as it takes."

***

The sun's light on his face woke Kormak. He had slept on the sterncastle wrapped in his cloak. Rhiana stood nearby, hand cupped over her eyes, looking into the distance.

"They will spot the Kraken's ships soon," she said.

Kormak pulled himself upright. "You think?"

"I know." She sounded certain. He did not bother to ask her how she could be. She had senses other than he did and she could use those of her familiar too, no doubt.

The lookout cried *sail ho* from overhead. Zamara shouted orders. The drums started beating, summoning the crew to their battle stations. Frater Jonas stepped up to the sterncastle and began to bless them all. For once the sailors stopped swearing and mouthed the words of the prayers. At such a time it did not hurt to make sure you stood in the Light of the Holy Sun. From force of habit, Kormak found himself saying the words himself.

Rhiana picked up a long spear she had brought. It looked like a harpoon. She tested its balance. She looked uneasy as the crew made their devotions.

***

Ahead of them the sleek lines of the Ocean's Blade pierced the horizon. Someone aboard the ship had noticed the pursuit. Its many oars moved like the legs of a centipede as the trireme came round to face them.

It brought its ram into attack position and narrowed the ship's profile, making it a harder target for their missile weapons. It came to Kormak that they could lose this fight even if they won it. If the beak of the ram stove in their sides, the Sea Dragon would go down along with its prey. They would never make it home to land.

A short distance from the Ocean's Blade lay the Kraken's Reach. It too was preparing for war. Men flooded onto its decks and began to man catapults and ballistae. The sea anchor was being hauled up and sail added as the ship swung around into a position to attack.

Kormak took a deep breath and ran through the calming exercises he had been taught back on Mount Aethelas. He would worry about such troubles when they happened.

More and more crossbowmen moved around him, taking up firing positions on the forecastle. The ballista was crewed. The acrid tang of alchemical fire made Kormak's mouth dry. Rhiana's nostrils flared in distaste. Incongruously the dolphin flashed from the water as if leaping with joy.

"No monsters coming?" Kormak shouted. His words were barely audible over the clamour on the deck.

Rhiana shook her head but her expression was strange. "There is something but it is far, far below us. Leviathan perhaps."

"Be sure to tell me if it rises," he said.

She smiled. "You'll be the first to know."

He stared off into the distance. "They are not running," he said.

"With the wind we have they could not get far," she said. "They will try and take the weather gauge away from us, move into a position where we are sailing against the wind and where their oars give them the advantage."

Kormak understood at once. The Ocean's Blade had sweeps but the Sea Dragon was much larger, slower and more cumbersome, more like a floating castle than the long, sleek war-machine they faced. The trireme's course would take it past them and to the south.

Zamara bellowed at the helmsman and the prow began to sweep round. The Ocean's Blade changed its course too. Kormak noticed its sails had been taken down and it was now moving completely under oar-power. Against the wind, sails would only be a disadvantage. And again, it made the ship less of a target.

The engine crew shouted to each other and began to adjust the tension of the ropes on the ballista. They loaded an alchemical shell. The engine commander bellowed an order and the great arm swept forward, sending its missile arcing through the air towards the Ocean's Blade. It fell short and the engine commander nodded, undismayed. He had just been trying to find the range.

Rhiana looked pale and tense. Her eyes narrowed. The long slits in her throat were sealed so tight as to be almost invisible.

Kormak's hand toyed with the hilt of his sword. He kept it sheathed from force of habit. He would not draw it until a foe stood in front of him.

He flexed his knees, his movement in time with the vessel's as he prepared himself to fight on the unsteady deck. From behind them, Zamara's voice boomed out, giving orders, adjusting the course of the ship, to keep the distance between the two craft closing.

The catapult fired again.

The war-engine on the sterncastle joined in to bracket the trireme with fire. By accident or design, the war-galley turned tightly and began to come straight at them, avoiding both shots. The *boom-boom-boom* of its drums rolled across the water. Its oars moved in unison and it surged forward. It was going to ram.

Kormak took another deep calming breath. The Sea Dragon rolled in the swell. The galley raced closer. The second of the Kraken's ships altered course. Its siege engines fired, sending huge rocks tumbling through the air. As they splashed into the nearby water huge spouts leapt into the air.

Rhiana's knuckles went white on the shaft of her spear. Frater Jonas kept up his prayers from the rear of the ship. The war-engines fired at the Ocean's Blade once more. One of the jars of alchemical fire hit. The warriors on the Sea Dragon roared triumphantly but nothing happened.

Perhaps the flask had failed to break, or perhaps its contents had proven to be inert. The intensity of the drumbeat from the trireme increased. The ship surged through the water, the great beak of the ram breaking the waves into a foaming mass.

Within heartbeats it was within crossbow range. The command to fire rang out. A hail of crossbow bolts flickered between the two ships. The pirate crew crouched out of line of fire. Towards the rear and on the sterncastle a few were visible from the elevated height of the Sea Dragon's forecastle. The arrows scythed down on some but men with shields protected the helmsman and the captain. Kormak could see no sign of the Kraken.

Smoke rose from the decks of the Ocean Blade. Perhaps the ballista shot was taking effect after all. Less than two hundred strides of open water separated the two ships now. The ram aimed at the Sea Dragon like a great spear.

A massive rock tumbled out of the sky over the Sea Dragon. Wood splintered near Kormak. Men screamed. He heard howling and whimpering from nearby and saw a man lying crushed where a huge piece of shot had landed. It had driven a hole in the deck and the man's broken body lay beneath it. Blood turned the deck around him red.

The Sea Dragon's war-engines fired again. One shot missed. Another shot hit the Ocean's Blade. This one erupted into a conflagration. Perhaps it had hit a pot of lantern oil.

Flames ran along the deck of the ship. Burning men leapt into the water, their bodies outlined by halos of green flame. Jumping into the water did not extinguish the fire. They sank into the depths still surrounded by the baleful alchemical glow.

Another hail of crossbow bolts flickered out at the oncoming galley. One struck a shield-bearer and sent him screaming to the ground. Another hit the helmsman. He slumped over the wheel. His weight moved the Ocean's Blade's rudder. It swept out of the line of its attack run.

The oars no longer rose and fell with a regular rhythm. Pirates leapt overboard, trying to get away from the flames. Some of the oarsmen, braver, drunker or more crazy than the rest, kept rowing. In the confusion of the battle they probably had not yet realised what had happened.

Zamara altered the course of the Sea Dragon. The great ship heeled round as the galley moved closer. It was not just the remaining oarsmen keeping it going—it was pure momentum.

The Ocean's Blade burned from end to end. More and more of the crew jumped overboard.

Even crewless the galley would be deadly. The ram would not even have to bite deep. It would just need to hit them and have the flames spread to the Sea Dragon's pitch-soaked timbers.

Another massive rock smashed into the Sea Dragon's sails. The canvas tore with a ripping noise so loud it sounded like a scream.

Zamara bellowed more commands. The war-engines turned on their pivots to face the second pirate ship. The crossbow men strode across the deck to new firing positions. Kormak glanced over to see how far away the second enemy ship was.

Not so close yet. There would be more missile fire before any conflict. He glanced back at the blazing trireme. It was only thirty strides away now.

Twenty strides. He could feel the heat coming from the floating bonfire. Another man leapt overboard, screaming, covered in flame.

Ten strides. The Ocean's Blade was so close now that the fire might leap between one ship and the other. Kormak held his breath.

The galley slid by the prow of the Sea Dragon as the great cog completed its turn. Its oars no longer moved. It was losing momentum. Soon it would be a floating funeral pyre for the men who had died aboard it. Kormak smelled the stink of their burning flesh now.

The second pirate ship bore down on them. It was even larger than the Sea Dragon. Armed men crowded its rigging. They lined its sides, howling battle cries, shouting challenges and obscenities. The engine crews kept a rain of missiles arcing between the ships. The Sea Dragon no longer lobbed alchemical fire. Zamara did not want to risk a collision with a burning vessel.

It was obvious the pirates wanted to get to grips with them and take them as a prize. It was equally obvious Zamara wanted to do the same to them. Kormak looked at Rhiana. She smiled, not afraid but wary.

Kormak studied the twisted faces of the screaming pirates and remembered the dead of Wood's Edge, the raped woman, the men and children with their throats cut. He thought of all the other places he had seen devastated by men such as these. He did not bother to force his anger down. He let it warm him. He welcomed the coming conflict.

The two ships came together with a mighty crash. Pirates vaulted over the railings and swung from mast to mast using the guy ropes of the sails. They came over with swords in their hands and daggers between their teeth.

At an order from Terves, the marines raised their shields and formed a solid line. They met the pirates with the discipline of first rate line infantry. They blocked blows with their shields and stabbed through the gaps with their swords. The crossbowmen kept firing into the enemy ship. Some pirates returned fire with a mixture of spears, darts and bolts.

Kormak took a moment to assess the situation. The pirates outnumbered them. The Sea Dragon had taken a beating while Zamara dealt with the trireme. The pirates charged with as unnatural savagery and no concern for their own lives.

Someone dropped out of the rigging above him, smiling, brought a long curved blade down towards his head. He stepped away, unsheathed his own blade from the scabbard and took the man's head off. It rolled away, dribbling blood, still smiling.

The sheer weight of the pirates pushed the marines back from the barrier. More of the enemy swung down from above to attack from the rear.

Kormak leapt down from the forecastle, booted feet crunching into the shoulders of a pirate, sending the man sprawling. Even as he struggled for balance, Kormak stabbed down, piercing his target through the heart.

He confronted a small group of pirates. His blade flickered out, removing a hand, an arm, penetrating a chest. In as many heartbeats he killed three men. The rest did not even blink but came on fighting.

Drugged, judging by the way their pupils were dilated, or under the influence of evil magic. The image of men still rowing even as alchemical fire burned their ship sprang into his mind. These pirates were not going to retreat and their morale was not going to break.

Zamara's marines had realised the same thing. Shouts of dismay went up under the berserker onslaught. Men slid in blood, tripped over loose entrails. The tight packed formation of the marines was breaking up.

The amulet on Kormak's breast warmed. There was magic at work here.

Rhiana dropped into place beside him, spear taking a pirate through the chest. Bubbles of bloody froth emerged from the man's lungs as he fell over, still trying to claw at her.

"There is a Quan here," she said. "Its magic is goading on our foes and undermining the morale of our allies."

Her face looked strained, as she struggled to resist the spell.

"We'd best do something about that then," Kormak said. "Where is it?"

"On the enemy ship," Rhiana said.

"Then let's kill it."

CHAPTER NINETEEN

KORMAK RACED UP the stairs to the command deck. Zamara fought there side by side with Frater Jonas. The captain's face was pale but not panicked. The Elder Signs he and Jonas wore shielded them from the enemy magic, but not from the madmen throwing themselves across the gap between the two ships.

Jonas had a knife in each hand. The hilts bulged and something that looked like black ink dripped from the tip. A number of dead men lay near the priest. They showed no fatal wounds.

Poison in the blades, Kormak thought. Bulbs in the hilts to inject it. A scratch would be fatal. The priest was a more dangerous man than Kormak had at first believed.

A pirate on a swinging line barrelled into Zamara, knocking him over. Kormak chopped down the corsair and stood over the captain as he pulled himself to his feet.

Kormak made sure that the captain was all right—without Zamara to guide the fight the crew would be overcome—then leapt across the gap onto the pirate ship. He tore through a group of reavers like a whirlwind of death.

Rhiana landed beside him and stabbed a man through the eye. Her prey fell back, still slashing. She hit him with the butt of the staff, breaking his nose and sending him reeling to the ground.

"Where?" Kormak asked.

A flicker of concentration passed across her face. "Above."

A long way above them black robes fluttered among the sails. He chopped down every man in his way until he reached the mast.

He sheathed his sword and pulled himself hand over hand up the rigging. It flexed under his weight, sending him swaying. The pirates in the crowsnests but were too busy sniping at the decks of the Sea Dragon with their crossbows to pay much attention to him.

Kormak kept moving, wondering how long it would be before someone spotted him. All it would take would be one arrow. It would not even have to kill him, just make him lose his grip for a second. The deck lay a long way below.

Looking down he saw scores of pirates still swarming on the deck. The powerful sorcery of the Quan drove them to rage. The Siderean sailors faltered under its baleful mental influence. The protective amulet blazed against Kormak's chest.

His arms burned with the strain of climbing. The effort of hacking his way across the deck had cost him an enormous amount of energy. His lungs felt empty. No matter how hard he breathed it was difficult to get enough air into them.

The Quan floated above the mast, anchored there by two of its tentacles. He remembered the Kraken's long slow descent from the balconies back in Triturek. The Quan had similar magic, allowing it to float in air as easily as it floated in water.

He pulled himself up to where the cross-spar joined the mast. The monster did not appear to have spotted him but who knew what senses the creature possessed? He glanced down. Rhiana clambered up below him, slowed by the spear she held in one hand.

He drew his sword and ran out along the spar. About halfway to his target, the Quan's robes flowed and swirled. Its tentacles changed their grip and the squid-like head swung towards him. A strange glow blazed in the Quan's eyes. The Elder Sign grew even warmer against his chest as the creature concentrated its malevolent energies on him.

A moment before he reached it, the Quan's tentacles unwound from around the spar and it floated free in the air. Long sucker covered limbs lashed out at Kormak, attempting to push him into space.

He lashed out with his dwarf-forged blade, separating one tentacle from the Quan's torso. He struck again. The squid-like creature writhed bonelessly and eluded him. Something long and moist wrapped itself around Kormak's leg and tugged.

On the narrow piece of wood fifty strides above the deck, he could not keep his balance. He started to fall. He grabbed the creature with his left hand and stabbed upwards into the cowl of the robe with the blade in his right. If he fell to his doom on the deck below he was damn well taking the creature with him.

Rhiana's spear drove through the Quan's body. A hissing scream filled the air. The black robes bulged and shrank as the monster writhed like a serpent in its death throes.

He struggled to hold on to the squirming mass of rubbery flesh as it fell.

He dropped slowly—the same magic that kept the Quan in the air helped slow his descent too. Faces looked up.

The sailors pointed up at the apparition descending upon them. The Quan's evil spell was broken. The combatants looked like men woken from a strange nightmare. The berserk madness had vanished from the pirate's faces. The Siderean marines no longer looked riven by self-doubt and fear.

Many wore a puzzled expression. For a moment it looked as if they would stop fighting altogether but then Zamara bellowed an order and the marines returned to the fray. Attacking their still confused opponents, they drove the pirate's back towards the railings on the edge of the deck.

A crossbowman took aim at Kormak. Before the pirate pulled the trigger, Kormak let go. A sickening sensation of free-fall hit his stomach. He gripped the hilt of his dwarf-forged sword with both hands and lashed out, piercing the sail. The razor edge ripped the fabric. He twisted the blade to create drag, slowing his descent.

The crossbow bolt flickered overhead and buried itself in the body of the Quan. The monster still thrashed, its unnatural vitality animating it long after a man would have sunk into death.

The wooden deck rose to meet Kormak. The last part of the sail gave way and he fell. He hit the deck rolling. As he came to his feet, he chopped down the nearest pirate.

He stood behind the mass of the sea-reavers. He stabbed the nearest one in the back and then hacked his way through the rest. Disoriented by the removal of the Quan's spell, assaulted from behind, and seeing their comrades fall, the pirates panicked.

It was a turning point.

Soon the pirates were dead or driven into the sea and the marines vaulted between the two ships to claim the pirate vessel. The corpse of the Quan lay quiescent on the deck. The marines stood guard over the captured pirates and Zamara strode the command deck of his prize smiling in triumph.

Rhiana dropped down from the rigging. She pulled her harpoon from the Quan's corpse then drove it home again and again. She kept stabbing until green ichor flowed and the Quan lost all shape.

***

The Kraken was nowhere to be found among his crew. Questioning revealed that he had disappeared into the water earlier along with two of the Quan. None of the pirates believed him drowned. They had seen him do such things before.

Rhiana nodded her head as if this confirmed something that she already knew. Zamara lost his earlier jubilation and became pensive. Frater Jonas frowned and offered up prayers to the Holy Sun for their protection. Kormak suspected that in his mind's eye, the priest saw another gigantic squid rising from the deep to smash their ships to smithereens.

Or something even worse—Leviathan.

"What shall we do now?" Zamara asked. "Wait here for the sorcerer to return to the surface?"

"If he returns," Kormak said. "There is no guarantee he's going to do that any time soon. And if he does he may be in the sort of company we cannot defeat."

"If he finds what he looking for down there," Rhiana said, "he will come back with the power to destroy us all."

Zamara said, "Since none of us have mastered the difficult art of water breathing—except, of course, you, my lady—we don't have many options. We either wait here for him to return to the surface or we depart and hope that he does not manage to waken the beast."

As he spoke his eyes never left the recumbent form of the Quan.

"You mean run away?" Jonas said. There was no mockery in his tone. He sounded like he thought flight might be a good idea.

"Not while there is still a chance of stopping him," Kormak said.

Rhiana looked at Kormak. Before she opened her mouth he knew what she was going to say. "We have the ancient armour. Someone could come down with me and find out exactly what the Kraken is up to."

Her tone of voice made it obvious that no matter whether anyone accompanied her or not she was going to go.

"If there are more Quan down there the two of you will be going to your death," Jonas said. His tone made it quite clear he was not volunteering himself.

Kormak considered his options. Rhiana wanted him to go with her. It was an act almost foolhardy bravery to seek the Kraken and his allies in their own element. Memories of being trapped in the tunnel into the pirate's mansion flooded back. His heart started to pound. He did not want to go but he knew that if he did not, it would be the beginning of the end for him. He could not shirk his duties simply because he was afraid.

"I will go down with you," he said.

"You will need to leave your amulets behind," she said. "You might have been able to survive for a short time with them impairing the armour's functions but there is no way you can reach the ocean's bottom with that happening. Your life will be entirely dependent on the armour working perfectly."

"Very well," Kormak said. "You're the expert in these matters and I will take your word for it."

"Then let us get ready," Rhiana said. "We have wasted enough time as it is."

CHAPTER TWENTY

THE ANCIENT ARMOUR encased Kormak's chest. Energy tingled on his skin.

Rhiana walked around him, making adjustments, checking all the seals were in place. Frater Jonas stood nearby watching everything. The deadly fighting man so briefly revealed had disappeared back into the priest's nervous looking form.

Kormak slid the scabbard of the dwarf-forged blade over his shoulder. Rhiana believed that so long as the weapon did not touch the armour, it would cause no problems.

The metal and crystal helmet weighed heavy in his hands. He was counting on it to let him breathe in the deepest water. He took a deep breath and cleared his mind of fear. The effect only lasted a moment before nervousness started to niggle away at the edges of his consciousness.

He was going into the depths of the ocean, a place he knew nothing about, to face foes adapted to thrive there. According to the sailors on the Kraken's Reach, two Quan still accompanied the sorcerer.

"Ready?" Rhiana asked. Kormak considered making a joke. Instead he took another deep breath and nodded and said, "Yes. I am."

"I'm glad somebody is," Rhiana said. "It troubles me that a surface dweller should be more prepared to go beneath the waves than I am."

Captain Zamara and his crew looked on. They were all glad they did not have to do what he was doing. Looking at the water's glittering surface, it came to him that he wastrusting his life to an ancient artefact that had almost killed him on the only previous occasion he had worn it.

Kormak placed the helmet upon his head. He could still hear the crew's speech but it sounded distant. His realised he was holding his breath.

He forced himself to relax and exhale. He could no longer catch the scent of the sea or the odour of his companions. He could not smell blood or excrement or any of the other aromas that filled the air over the ship after the battle. There was a smell almost like mint.

Rhiana looked at him and said, "We'd best get going."

She stepped up onto the guard-rail and dropped into the water. The waves closed above her head with a splash.

Kormak shrugged and vaulted over the barrier, bringing his feet together so that he entered the water cleanly. A moment of panic hit him as he sank. Murk replaced brilliant oceanic sunlight. The Holy Sun's rays penetrated the water as if breaking through the canopy of a forest.

The barnacle-encrusted keel of the ship receded above him. The bubbling sound caused by his descent filled his ears.

Rhiana swung around him with an eerie grace, much more at home in the water than on land. She moved like a seal, circling around him and smiling.

The gills in her throat opened and closed as they processed the ocean water. Faint white trails emerged from them and bubbled towards the surface.

He raised his hand and waved to her. He felt slow and clumsy, his movements impeded by the thickness of the water. Once again he held his breath and once again he had to force himself to exhale and inhale. His heart beat against his ribs like a drum. He offered up a prayer to the Holy Sun that this ancient armour would continue to work.

We need to get going downwards, said a faint voice inside his head. It took him a moment to realise that it was not his own thoughts and he felt a surge of panic. He concentrated on visualising an Elder Sign to repel the intrusion.

Rhiana shook her head. *I am speaking to you with my mind.* Her voice sounded much more distant and the words were much harder to comprehend. *I can only do that with your cooperation. And I am going to need that once we reach our destination.*

Kormak wondered whether she could read his thoughts or riffle through his memories and ferret out his secrets. Such a thing had happened in the past when he had faced the Stealer of Flesh.

Can you understand my thoughts? He felt strange and self-conscious concentrating on the words. When he got no response, he made a gesture to his own head and then mouthed the words. She smiled as if she understood.

I can only broadcast to you. I cannot read your mind. However if you speak normally, I will be able to make out your words. You have air in your lungs and you can use your vocal chords.

For how much longer, Kormak wondered.

The open sky seemed very distant and waters dark and chill swirled all around him.

***

He dropped towards the ocean floor. Rhiana continued to circle. The ships above them receded, becoming shadowy outlines against the light of the Sun. A finned shape moved closer. Kormak saw a dolphin, most likely the one that had followed them all this way out into the ocean, Rhiana's familiar.

He flailed his limbs and stopped for a moment, kicking his legs and moving his arms to maintain his position and orientate himself. He did not want simply to drop into the darkness. He needed control over what was happening to him.

Rhiana swam closer to him and placed her hand against the runes on the armour's chestplate. A look of concentration passed across her face. A faint vibration shivered the armour and then he began to move without any effort on his part. The sea behind him had become a white mass of bubbles.

When he stretched his arms he met some resistance, as if the drag of his own limbs impeded his movement. He placed them over his head, pointing them like a diver about to enter the water and his speed increased. He discovered that he could guide his direction by altering the angle at which he held his arms and by twisting his legs. It was as if a great hand pushed him along and all he had to do was show it which way to go. Rhiana swam alongside him, no longer keeping up quite so easily.

There is a spell-engine within the armour that enables it to move as well as to provide you with air.

"Does it have any other tricks?" Kormak asked. She reached out and touched the side of the helmet. A beam of light scythed out into the gathering darkness, illuminating a tunnel through the gloomy water.

He touched the side of the helmet where she had and the light winked out. He touched it again and the light came back. He resisted smiling like a child given a new toy. He made the light vanish once more.

He touched the breastplate of the armour and ran his fingers along the pattern in the reverse of the way that she had. The vibration ceased and he stopped moving. He repeated her action and he once more began to move. This time he did smile. Powerful ancient magic was at work here.

I see that you're getting the hang of it. That is good.

"I can see why you were so keen to get this armour back," Kormak said. "It is worth a fortune to the right man."

The dolphin swam alongside them. It opened its snout and a high-pitched clicking noise came out. Rhiana nodded. *We need to be on our way.*

Kormak followed her down towards the ocean's bed.

***

Rhiana produced her green glowing pearl for the waters became darker and darker as they made their way down. It was dim as twilight and became more shadowy the deeper they went. Kormak summoned the light from the armour's helmet once again.

It became more and more difficult to move his limbs. The armour creaked and groaned as if under pressure from an enormous vice. Rhiana gestured for him to stop and moved closer to him. She inspected the breastplate with an anxious look on her face. She then made a similar inspection on the helmet.

"Is something wrong?" Kormak asked.

She did not respond. She ran her fingers along the crystal of the visor, perhaps seeking out for tiny cracks. Kormak kept quiet. If something went wrong with the armour at this depth, there was no way he could make it to the surface again. He would run out of air long before he could do so.

I think it's all right. The pressure has not damaged the armour.

"You think it's all right," Kormak said. "I am reassured."

If it fails, you'll be dead before you know it so there's no point in worrying.

"I think I could somehow manage to worry about that," Kormak said.

I just wanted to check. I thought I saw something but it seems I was just imagining it.

Kormak wished that he could really hear her voice. It would have been much easier to judge whether she was lying on not. Her projections into his mind all came in a flat neutral tone.

She gestured downwards. The dolphin had stopped frolicking and seemed to be saving its energy. It pushed itself onwards with a lazy flick of its tail.

***

They reached the ocean floor.

He had been expecting the sort of flat sand that he remembered seeing when swimming underwater near a beach. This was more like flying above the slopes of the mountains in his native land of Aquilea. He supposed that an island was only a mountain whose peak had broken out above the surface of the waves.

Shoals of fish shimmered into view, unlike anything he had seen closer to the surface. Some were very large and had jaws that could take off a limb as easily as a shark.

"How do you know where we are going?" Kormak asked.

There is something below us. Something very powerful. It broadcasts like a foghorn would to your ears, to my senses.

"I can sense nothing," Kormak said. "But I suppose that is hardly surprising."

You are lucky. It is a most disturbing presence. Like nothing I have ever encountered. It is something truly alien. Like a Quan but unlike one. It is very powerful and yet... She broke off as if struggling to express a concept she did not have the words for.

It is no use. I cannot tell you exactly what it is about this thing that disturbs me so much. In any case, you'll see it soon for yourself. We are almost there.

He realised that they had not been following the ridgelines by accident. They were like men creeping through the hills, using the lay of the land to avoid being seen. He wondered if whatever it was down there perceived Rhiana the way she detected it. He began to wonder whether it had spotted him. Just because he could not sense something did not mean that the reverse was true.

He shook his head, sending the light beam from the helmet skittering everywhere. A man could drive himself mad with such thoughts. He swam lower, skimming over the slopes, taking advantage of any cover that they provided. The lights provided by his armour and her jewel would make them visible to any watcher anyway so was all a bit pointless. Instinct kept him seeking concealment anyway.

They breasted the ridge. Beneath them lay something gigantic. In places only shadowy outlines were visible. Other parts glowed with a luminescence of their own. It looked like the body of an enormous crustacean combined with that of the largest squid that had ever existed. It took a long moment for the scale of the thing to really sink in.

It was bigger than a small town. One sweep of those tentacles could do more than sink a ship. It could smash a castle.

"It's a monster," he said.

It is a Leviathan. This time Kormak caught something of the wonder and terror in her tone. Horror and awe transfigured her face.

Kormak hovered above the thing wondering what he could do against such a beast. A hundred war-engines throwing alchemical fire would barely make an impression on such a thing. He looked around to see if he could see any of the Quan.

There was nothing, not even seaweed or any form of reef. Every living thing in the area gave the monster a wide berth.

We need to get inside. The Leviathan was not just the Mother of the Quan, it was their home, a vessel in which they lived.

This creature was a ship of sorts, a living engine. It was one thing to listen to tales about it. It was another to be confronted by the reality.

What could have made it? Or had it been born and shaped by sorcery? It was easy to imagine something growing to this vast size in the depths of the ocean but how had it been fed? What was there in all creation that could provide prey for such a thing?

It devoured life. It swept up everything in its path, the way a whale takes down krill. The Quan helped feed it. A portion of every life they took went to Leviathan. Or so the Elders taught me.

Kormak imagined this giant sweeping through the depths, disgorging thousands of Quan to reave and slay. He imagined it birthing giant squids and other monsters. He had a brief vision of the wars of the elder world titans, the only ones who could stand against such a thing. He doubted anything in the world today could defeat this thing if it sprang to life.

The Kraken means to wake Leviathan.

"Now that is a frightening thought," Kormak said.

We had best see if we can stop it happening.

CHAPTER TWENTY-ONE

THEY SWEPT OVER the drowned hillsides of the monster, passing above tentacles larger than the walls of some towns, heading towards the huge shell at the rear of the Leviathan.

Nearness obscured the outline of the vast creature, made impossible to perceive in its entirety. Instead he noticed the components. Segmented tentacles, like the armoured bodies of massive worms, formed ridges along the sea bottom. The great carapace resembled the side of a mountain covered in luminescent algae. The edges measured twenty strides thick.

Darkness shadowed a vast area where the shell had blistered and flowed. No algae glowed there. Kormak guessed they were swimming on the edges of the wound caused by whatever weapon Tritureon had used to defeat Leviathan. This huge crater was the result of that mighty stroke. He wondered at the power of something that capable of harming a creature the size of Leviathan. A surge of awe passed through him at the thought of its wielder. The Old Ones had fought wars on a scale near unimaginable to mortal men.

All he could see of Rhiana was the faint bobbing glow of the green pearl. He followed in her wake, along with the dolphin, dropping into a cold shadow of the mountainous creature. Openings pitted the huge carapace. Up ahead lay one such grotto. A Quan emerged from within it.

No black robes shrouded this one's body. Its body expanded and contracted in pulses as it moved through the water. It hovered in the water, its glowing eyes fixed on him. His vision swirled and rippled as if a huge current swept through the ocean depths around him.

Thousands of Quan spewed forth from hundreds of orifices in the Leviathan's side. All of their eyes glowed with evil hunger and all of them swept towards him with deadly intent. These monsters were huge, their tentacles long and strong, their beaks sharp as a steel blade.

His heart raced. His mouth went dry. He was going to die here, his armour shredded by this unstoppable army. He would drown while they feasted on his soul.

Amid the flood of panicked thoughts a small part of him noticed how unusual this fear was, so much more intense than anything normal.

From force of habit, he took a deep calming breath and reached for his blade.

He envisioned an Elder Sign, recited the protective prayers he had learned on Mount Aethelas. The great horde of sea demons became wraith-like, all except one. It floated in front of him, reaching out with long muscular tentacles, intent on wrapping his helmeted head in an obscene caress.

He drew his blade. With the resistance of the water it came clear of the scabbard more slowly than normal.

It did not matter. Sharper by far than any razor, the blade sliced through the tentacle, sending it dropping to the sea bottom.

A cloud of black ink swirled out from the Quan, obscuring the blood, making the monster invisible.

He aimed at where the Quan had last been but hit nothing.

He forced himself to advance through the inky murk, worried that if he used the armour's full speed he would smash headlong into the side of the Leviathan and crack the faceplate.

Every second he feared that a long tentacle would enwrap him from some unexpected direction. Visions of armies of translucent Quan still filled his mind. The fact that he saw them in the murk emphasised their unreality.

The cloud thinned out. Ribbons of clear water gnawed at its edges. He emerged into the phosphorescent shadow of the Leviathan. Something strong and serpent-like looped around him, immobilising his sword arm.

A heavy weight pressed against his back.

Suckers attached themselves to the crystal of his faceplate, obscuring his vision.

Fear returned, amplified by the fact that he was in the grip of his foe. He struggled with all his strength, trying to break the monster's hold. The thing that he fought flexed but did not give way.

The armour creaked. Panic clawed at him. If the Quan succeeded in damaging the armour...

He twisted his legs, arched his back. The armour changed direction, heading for the wall of the Leviathan. He turned so that the Quan cushioned the shock of impact. Its body distorted from the pressure and its grip slackened on his sword arm. His blade bit into the Quan's flesh. More inky stuff filled the water but this time it was blood. The dye reservoirs within the creature's body must have been drained by its previous efforts.

The Quan let him go and he twisted to lash out at it as it fled. His blade penetrated the creature's eye and it ceased to move.

Another Quan floated in the water. Rhiana hovered near it, along with her dolphin familiar. He caught the merest flicker of what was projected. The rituals that protected his mind against the Quan's psychic attack made it impossible for him to hear her at this range. He did not care. He was not about to let himself become vulnerable once again.

She swam over and placed her mouth against the crystal visor, a gesture of peculiar intimacy. "I am surprised you managed to fight at all. My foe almost overwhelmed me with its visions. That thing was very strong."

Kormak said, "Can you find the Kraken?"

She shook her head. "Something is waking inside the Leviathan. I am guessing that if we head towards it, we will find him."

They swam into the grotto from which the Quan had emerged. Semi-translucent pods barnacled the walls. Within each huddled a Quan. All of the creatures' eyes were closed and all of their limbs drooped within their integuments. Here was the army he had seen in his vision made flesh, if a way could be found to unleash them.

As they swam through the long spiralling corridor, moving inwards, they passed hundreds and hundreds of the monsters. They were everywhere, on the walls, on the ceiling. Some of them were larger, some of them were smaller.

"Are they sleeping?" Kormak asked. He relaxed his mental defences for a moment.

Not sleeping. Waiting to be born.

An image flickered through his mind. Of all those thousands of eyes opening at once. Of all those thousands of tentacles stretching out to enfold him.

He felt a pressure in his mind, a sense of something vast and horrific waiting ahead of them. The lights intensified, slowly.

The Leviathan is waking. The Kraken is rousing it.

***

They emerged from a pool. Water streamed from Rhiana's mouth. She coughed. The dolphin flipped itself into the air.

The resistance of the water around Kormak vanished as he waded up onto the floor of air-filled chamber. Something sticky sucked at the boots. More of the Quan pods hung on the walls, but these ones looked dried out and dead.

"What is this?" Kormak asked. His words reverberated inside the helmet and echoed around the cavernous chamber.

"The air is breathable here," Rhiana said. Kormak did not remove his helmet.

They pushed on into the cavernous chamber filled with statues. Most of them depicted a creature partially human and partially Quan, with a squid-like head super-imposed on a web-footed and web-clawed humanoid body.

Kormak studied their surroundings. "I believe these are the chambers of Dhagoth, grown out of the living flesh of the ship. Maybe the Leviathan filters air out of water the way that armoured suit does. Or like your gills."

"Why would an Old One need air?"

"To work magic? To speak spells? Or for reasons we will never understand. They do not think like we do."

Kormak raised the visor of the ancient armour and sniffed. The air smelled fusty and damp. Something stank like rotten fish. It made him feel nauseous but he was still glad to feel the air on his face. He closed his eyes from moment and dismissed the image of the huge

190 | WILLIAM KING

weight of water above his head. Standing inside this enclosed area, squinting into the odd luminescence created by the huge living organism, he felt further from safety than he ever had before.

"Are you all right?" Rhiana asked. "You look a little strange."

Kormak grinned. "It's this place that is strange. I am still trying to get my head around where we are and what we are doing here."

"Then you'd better do so quickly—you can't go wandering around with your eyes closed in a place like this."

From force of habit Kormak's hand moved to where his Elder Sign should have been. After so many years he felt naked without it. At least, he still had his sword. He glanced around the chamber and noticed cloth hangings, covered in delicate embroidery. They depicted scenes similar to the ones seen back in Triturek. These ones depicted the triumph of the Quan over their amphibian adversaries, showed them in positions suggestive of reverence floating around their human-bodied, squid-headed deity.

"I don't like this place," Rhiana said.

"That just shows you're sensible," Kormak replied.

He inspected the tapestry. The weaving was intricate, the creation of more than human patience and skill. He had seen such work in other times and other places. It was very definitely the work of an Old One.

He let go of the cloth. He was putting off their advance. He dreaded the prospect of meeting the Kraken.

He squared his shoulders, touched the hilt of his blade and said, "Let's go."

***

The corridor became even larger, the ceiling three times the height of a man. There was an organic quality to their surroundings. The walls were ridged as if ribs lay beneath. He reminded himself that he was not looking at stone but at the carapace or skeleton of a living thing.

More of the Quan pods appeared on the walls but they looked flabby. The translucent membrane had collapsed. The things inside were decayed.

"Are you sure we are going in the right direction," Kormak said.

"We are moving towards the strongest source of magic," she said. "That will have to do."

The corridor emerged onto a balcony looking overlooking a massive cavern. Long ramps flowed down to the floor of the chamber. They had the same organic look as the rest of the internal architecture of the Leviathan.

In the centre of the chamber the Kraken waited, standing beside something that resembled a cross between a coral reef and a human brain. Driven into its centre was a large gem that looked like the Teardrop of Leviathan only much larger.

Mounted on the breastplate of the Kraken's armour the Teardrop itself glowed with a brilliant light that was absorbed by the brain-like structure. It dimmed and brightened with a regular rhythm as stable as that of a heartbeat.

"He's using that gem to bring the Leviathan to wakefulness," Rhiana said, her eyes wide with wonder and horror. The sorcerer gave them a mocking wave, welcoming them like old friends. In his hand the lightning rod Kormak remembered from the encounter in the pirate's palace sparked.

"You may as well come down," the Kraken said. His voice filled the space, echoing through all the nooks and crannies within the chamber. "I'm glad to have somebody else here. You will be witnesses to the dawn of a new age. Hell, if you're not too much trouble, I will even spare your lives."

Kormak wondered whether this was part of some scheme to delay them until his sorcery was complete. In any case, the Kraken's invitation was not to be declined. It might give them a chance to get within striking distance without being blasted by a spell. Without his amulets he could do little to prevent that.

Rhiana took the left hand ramp and Kormak took the right. At least that way they could not both be struck by the same spell.

The glow of magic underlit the Kraken's features. His lips drew back in a ghastly smile that made his face skull-like. The greenish luminescence of the gem reflected in his eyes so that they seemed to be lit from within by evil magic.

He went on speaking, a man wanting to share his triumph. "It has taken me a lifetime to get to this place. You have no idea of the sacrifices I made."

Kormak said nothing. He did not want to break the spell of recollection that the sorcerer wove around himself.

"Some of the sacrifices you made I knew," Rhiana said. "My sister Mika, for one."

There was a world of pain in her voice.

The sorcerer laughed. "I won't lie to you. I won't tell you that I am sorry. I did what I needed to do to achieve my destiny."

"And what would that destiny be?" Rhiana said. "What was worth torturing and killing all those people?"

"I am the rightful King of Siderea. I will have my throne. And once I have that throne I will lead Siderea into a new age of glory. You don't understand what is happening here. You have no idea of the power that I am waking."

"You're bringing the Leviathan out of its long sleep," Rhiana said.

The sorcerer nodded, a teacher showing approval to a student who would prove to be brighter than he expected.

"Sleep is perhaps the wrong word. As is death. The Leviathan is in a state between the two. She no longer had the power to wake. She was crippled when Tritureon struck her with the stolen weapons of the Angels. The backlash drove her into a death-like slumber. She has had long strange aeons in which to heal.

"Dhagoth trapped the Leviathan's soul within the gem and bound her with pieces of resonant aether embedded in her hide, all slaved to the power of the Teardrop. Tritureon took the Teardrop as his spoils but he did not live long enough to enjoy them. The strain of using the forbidden weapons killed him not long after his hour of triumph. The secret of the Teardrop was preserved by Dhagoth's priestesses, of whom my mother was the last. She knew that with it she could wake Leviathan and control her. That secret was her legacy to me and I will make the best use of it.

"It will make me master of the world."

CHAPTER TWENTY-TWO

"YOU DON'T SERIOUSLY think you can control this monster?" Rhiana asked.

"Dhagoth did. By means of these gems. My mother taught me the rituals. She had been studying these things her entire life. I only regret that she did not live to see me achieve this goal. She never quite recovered from the poisons that my father's assassins used on her."

"You are not an Old One," Kormak said.

The sorcerer smiled and when he spoke his tone was mocking, "And few are better placed to know that than you, eh Guardian? I'm rather surprised that you allowed yourself to be hired as an assassin. I always believed that your Order was above such things."

"My Order does what needs to be done to ensure that the Law is not broken."

"Alas, once this ritual is complete your Order will be in no position to do anything to me. Oh, they will try but they will have my new army to contend with. Believe me, there is no power remaining in this world able to stand against it. Dhagoth's children are innumerable and the Leviathan can always breed more. You have seen what a few of them can do. I will soon have an army."

Kormak imagined an army of the squid-like monsters unleashed on the world. With their sorcery they would be very difficult to stop. It had taken the strength of one of the mightiest of the Old Ones and his chosen people to defeat them in ancient days. There was nothing left in the world with that kind of power. He thought of the vision he had seen surging through his mind when the Quan had unleashed its power against him. No human force could stand against it.

"You are beginning to understand," the Kraken said. "And I can assure you an army of Quan will be the least of my servants. Leviathan herself will be with me and there is no fleet in the world that she cannot destroy."

"And you are prepared to unleash an army of monsters against humanity simply to satisfy your ambition."

"In a word, yes," the Kraken said. "Although it is not mere vanity that motivates me. It is righteousness. I could not be a worse king than the present ruler of Siderea. I will be able to unify all the lands of men. I will be able to stand against the Shadow. I will be able to build an empire the like of which the Solari only dreamt of."

"You don't lack for ambition," Kormak said.

"It is not merely a dream. I will soon have the power to make it reality. By the way, I don't think you should come any closer. I really would prefer not to have to kill you or, indeed, give you the chance to kill me."

"I appreciate that," Kormak said. "Unfortunately you cannot be allowed to proceed."

"Why? What do you gain by attempting to stop me except quick and painful death?"

"We have managed to kill everything you sent against us so far," Rhiana said. "I don't think that you are any tougher than your servants."

"That is where you are wrong," the Kraken said. "I know how to work sorcery. I am protected by a Quan battle-harness. More to the point, I am connected to the Leviathan and an almost infinitely deep well of magical power."

He swept his fingers through the air, leaving a trail of sparks behind them and an after-image whose glow floated across Kormak's vision for moments afterwards. It was a display of compelling magical might. Kormak knew how difficult it was for sorcerer to summon power and the Kraken had done so with ease.

"I could slay you with a gesture," the Kraken said. "Please do not make me do so. I'm feeling quite sentimental and I would like to have some witnesses to my apotheosis. You will be my messengers to the world. Or you will die."

Rhiana edged towards the Kraken, keeping her spear up. Kormak stalked closer from the other side, trying to move past the edge of the sorcerer's peripheral vision, so that he could not target them both at once.

"You're going to be tiresome about this then," the Kraken said.

"I came here for vengeance," said Rhiana.

The Kraken smiled. "How very righteous of you. I am hardly one to criticise you for it though. I have spent my whole life seeking it."

There was sympathy in his manner. Rhiana's features hardened. She sprang forward, spear flickering out. The Kraken stepped to one side, almost too fast for the eye to follow. The power he drew from the gem made him much stronger and faster than a mortal man. He caught the haft of her spear with one hand and tore it from her grasp with the other.

Her knife was in her hand. She slashed his cheek. The Kraken grimaced. The skin beneath his eye peeled away, flopping down to reveal muscle and teeth then after a moment it knitted back together with no sign of scarring. He gestured again and a bolt of power emerged from his hand, smashing into Rhiana, hurling her backwards, her mouth open in a silent scream

Kormak sprang towards the Kraken. The sorcerer gestured with the lightning rod. A bolt of power danced from the wand's tip to the point of Kormak's blade. The shock ripped right up his arm but it was less than it had been back in the palace. His armour's gauntlets partially insulated him against the bolt. Nonetheless it was enough to set his fingers to spasming. The dwarf-forged blade dropped from his hand. The Kraken kicked it away and brought the rod down again. Kormak raised his arm to block the blow. The sleeve of his armour provided less protection against the blast than the gauntlet. His whole arm went numb. Sparks flickered on his field of vision. Strength drained from his body.

He tried to move but his legs refused to obey him. The Kraken raised the metal rod again and Kormak knew he would not survive the impact. Everything slowed for a moment. He was aware of everything: the beads of sweat on the Kraken's forehead, the faint hint of ozone in the air, the disappearing glow at the rod's tip and the fading runes on its side.

The death-blow began to descend.

Rhiana appeared behind the Kraken, her face pale, her eyes wide with shock. Her arm looped around the sorcerer's throat. Just for a moment, he was held immobile. Kormak forced his rubbery limbs to move, rolled away towards where his sword lay. The Kraken twisted his head to look Rhiana in the eye, just as he brought the tip of the wand into contact with her arm. It blazed less brightly this time. She screamed in agony but kept her grip tight, intent on squeezing all life out of her sister's killer.

"Enough," Kormak said. He drove his sword through centre of the Kraken's chest, smashing it through the Teardrop of Leviathan. There was a smell of burning. The runes on the dwarf-forged blade blazed bright red. The crystallised magic of the aether gem exploded outward. The Kraken's eyes went wide with agony. His lips twisted, revealing his brilliant white teeth gritted against each other. The aura around him intensified. A spark of the force struck Kormak.

Terrifying power surged into his mind bringing a thousand strange visions. He saw Dhagoth summoning the Leviathan from the depths. He saw him drive shards of the gem into her flesh and then use the remainder to control the beast and draw her soul into its heart. Now it was free.

The sorcerer's shout was agonised. "You fool! You don't know what you've done."

Part of Leviathan's soul had been imprisoned in the crystal. Now it was trying to return to its body. Hazy tendrils of power flickered through the air, flashing towards the coral brain. As they did so the walls around them began to vibrate.

The floor shifted beneath Kormak's feet. The monster was moving.

"The Leviathan is awake!" Rhiana shouted.

Kormak twisted the blade. The Kraken toppled, his features warped by horrible agony. The fall drove the sword in deeper. Rhiana let go to avoid the blade as it passed through the sorcerer's body. He forced himself upright and reached out.

Strong hands grasped at Kormak, clawing for his throat. He pulled back, but fingers dug into his windpipe.

The Kraken was choking him. Kormak let his weight fall forward and grabbed the chain on which the Teardrop had hung. He looped the chain around the Kraken's throat and sawed away, grinding the tightened metal links into the Kraken's windpipe like a garrotte. He drew blood. There was a whimper followed by an odd coughing sound. The grip on Kormak's throat lost its strength. The Kraken's face turned purple, his dreams of conquest vanishing as the tide of his life receded.

Kormak kept the pressure on until the sorcerer toppled.

He almost fell himself. He was still weak from the impact of the Kraken's lightning rod.

"We should get out of here." Rhiana said. She limped over to Kormak's side.

The whole chamber tipped over, sending them rolling towards the walls. Kormak heard a roaring noise in the distance. The floor vibrated beneath his feet.

"We can't go," he said. He picked up his blade and made his way towards the central brain node. "Not yet."

The aether released by the destruction of the Teardrop was settling. He lashed at the sparks with his blade and then drove it deep into the coral, cutting it. Once again a smell of burning filled the air. Kormak kept slashing, smashing nodes, severing ganglions, destroying every delicate thing he could find. The room continued to shiver and shake. Huge groaning, gurgling sounds filled the surrounding air.

From the sides of the room water poured in, great jets of it, spurting through the entranceway. Since the Leviathan had shifted, the sea must be filling the once-air-filled chambers.

Kormak pulled himself over to the Kraken's body and reached down for the ring. The Kraken's eyes opened and he looked at Kormak and then the piece of jewellery. A faint flicker of life was in his eyes. "It was my mother's," he said. "Don't take it now."

Just for a moment Kormak saw a little boy looking out through the dying man's eyes, gazing on the only token he had from his dead parent. He toyed with letting it rest with the corpse, but then he thought of all the people slaughtered at Woods Edge, of Rhiana's lost sister. He took his blade and cut off the Kraken's ring finger. As the light died from the sorcerer's eyes Kormak slipped the ring into his belt pouch.

The water rose until it was almost above his head.

"Time to go," Rhiana said. Kormak dropped the armours visor into position and sealed it, offering up a prayer to the Sun that its magic was still working.

They swam back the way they had come, through chambers filled with water. The priceless tapestries billowed like curtains of seaweed. The desiccated Quan corpses floated by. They exited through the vast crater and swam upwards. As they rose, Kormak saw the huge tentacles writhe, vast slow things, like gigantic dying sea serpents beating their brains out against the ocean floor, churning up gigantic swirling currents. Even as he watched they slowed and stopped. The luminescence that had once illuminated the beast's side was dimming.

At long last the strange death of the Leviathan was complete.

***

Kormak stood on the deck of the Sea Dragon. Overhead the stars were bright. Nearby he heard the soft footsteps of the night watch as they went about their business. Zamara was asleep on the command deck, wrapped in his cloak, the faithful Terves by his side.

Soft footfalls announced the presence of Rhiana. She came closer and laid a hand on his shoulder. "What are you going to do now?"

"Sail back to Siderea with Jonas and the captain; claim my share of the bounty. What about you?"

"I don't have much choice. I'll take the survivors of my crew back, see if we can pick up a smuggler back to the Pirate Islands."

The silence grew longer between them. "What about the armour?"

"It belongs to you. It always did. I just borrowed it."

"It's worth a lot of money to the right buyer."

"Well, at least you've turned a profit on this trip."

"It wasn't about profit," she said. "It was about repaying a debt."

"How do you feel about that?"

"Like I have laid down a heavy load. Like I can get back to being myself again."

"I'm glad."

She looked at the sword on his back. "You don't believe in putting down your burdens, do you?"

He shook his head and looked at the distant moon. It watched them like the eye of a mocking god. Somewhere ahead of them lay the coast of the Kingdoms of the Sun. He would be glad to get back.

THE END

ABOUT THE AUTHOR

William King lives in Prague, Czech Republic with his lovely wife Radka and his sons Dan and William Karel. He has been a professional author and games developer for almost a quarter of a century. He is the creator of the bestselling Gotrek and Felix series for Black Library and the author of the World of Warcraft novel *Illidan*. Over a million copies of his books are in print in English. They have been translated into 8 languages.

He has been short-listed for the David Gemmell Legend Award. His short fiction has appeared in Year's Best SF and Best of Interzone. He has twice won the Origins Awards For Game Design. His hobbies include role-playing games and MMOs as well as travel.

His website can be found at: www.williamking.me

Word-of-mouth is crucial for any author to succeed. If you enjoyed the book, please consider leaving a review, even if it's only a line or two; it would make all the difference and would be very much appreciated.

Made in the USA
Las Vegas, NV
25 February 2022